MURDER IN THE WINGS

The Shepton Rise Murders

D R JOHNSON

ISBN 978-1-0687858-1-8

The Shepton Rise Murders

1

Monday Morning.

An unseasonable cool breeze whips through the streets of Shepton Rise, blowing the blossom from the trees and carrying with it a general air of discontent. It's June, but you would hardly know it. Instead of dressing for the onset of summer and the promise of long days under blue skies, the townsfolk reach out for clothes they had put away for the winter, look up at grey clouds, and scowl. Those brave enough to hang out washing on the line find themselves scurrying outside again to rescue it from a sudden rain shower. No sooner have they draped their dripping clothes inside their houses, over radiators, clothes horses and the backs of chairs, than the sun, locked in a struggle with the easterly wind, will come out, tempting them to try again.

***

Feeling the chill in the air, Adam Broome pulled up the hood on his jacket, thankful that underneath his lumberjack shirt, he had put on his Talking Heads tee-shirt. He walked along the High Street, heading for the florist's shop.

This weather makes no sense! It's June, and I'm wearing three layers! he thought. Adam had recently rekindled a friendship with Ginny Fellows and had decided to call in to see her. Ginny wouldn't be expecting him, but he didn't want to arrive empty-handed, hence his visit to Bloomin' Marvellous.

Usually, the door would be wide open in the summer, but it was closed. The shop looked dark inside, but the windswept display of flowers outside suggested it was open. Adam pushed the door, which swung back with a bang, clattering against a metal bucket of roses. Adam froze, not just due to his noisy entrance but because of the unexpected scene before him. The owner, Samantha Drake, stood with one hand over her mouth and a pair of long scissors in the other. Adam followed her gaze. The shop was lined with flowers displayed in galvanised steel buckets. Protruding from between them, was a pair of legs, motionless on the concrete floor. Adam's heart skipped a beat; he feared the worst, but then he heard a sneeze, and Chris Current sat up. Samantha burst out laughing.

'Morning, Adam,' she said, 'Sorry for all the palaver. Chris is trying to fix a dodgy electrical socket but has hay fever and keeps sneezing. I've been trying not to giggle.'

'I thought I had stumbled into a murder scene. I reckoned you had done away with him.' Samantha pulled a menacing face, changed her hold on the scissors and made a stabbing motion.

'I can think of someone else I could bump off, but not Chris,' she laughed.

'I think I know who you mean,' chuckled Chris. 'And I'll help you do it. Anyway, that's you fixed, Samantha. You can turn the lights on now. I'll get off. I've got to replace an electric shower next. See you, Adam.'

Adam smiled as he watched Chris gather his tools and leave. Chris Current had been a few years below him at school, and unsurprisingly his nickname had been Sparks. How could he end up being anything other than an electrician?

'Now then, what can I do for you? Or should I say, do you in for?' smiled Samantha, waving the scissors.

'I wonder if you could help me choose some flowers for a friend? I don't want them to be overly romantic; we are just friends. Well, at the moment, anyway.'

***

"Unsettled conditions will continue into early June, with a changeable week ahead. Rain is likely at times, especially in the North and West, with below-average temperatures day and night."

'Oh! Oh...bother, Oh! Oh!...' Ginny turned off the radio in her office and searched for a suitable word to use as she surveyed the thirty manila folders which had been piled up on her desk but which had now toppled over and scattered across her office floor. She settled on 'Damn!' All the other expressions she could think of either sounded like the sort of things schoolgirls in the comics of her youth would say, or else they would be more at home on a building site! It wasn't exactly a calamity. After all, she could pile them all up again. Ginny smiled, remembering her childhood in this same High Street house, eagerly waiting for her comic, The Bunty, to pop through the letterbox. 'Oh, fiddlesticks!'

she said with a giggle, slapping the first folder down on the mahogany desk. It was the same desk that her father had worked at when she was a little girl. 'Oh, drat!' she placed another on top of it, 'Oh, blast!...Oh, crumbs!' Ginny could probably have carried on with this litany of polite expletives until she had rebuilt her towering pile of stationery but was interrupted by the sound of the doorbell ringing.

'Hello, Adam,' she smiled, 'What lovely Sweet Williams. Are they for me? Thank you. You've come just in time.'

'In time for what?' he asked, handing her the flowers.

'In time to distract me from doing my accounts and giving me an excuse to put the kettle on! Come on through!'

'Oh dear!' sighed Adam, looking at the mess on the office floor.

'I hadn't got around to using that expression yet,' Ginny laughed.

'I'll tidy this lot up while you make us a cup of tea,' said Adam, 'I want to get your opinion about something.'

Ten minutes later, Adam was squirming, rather than sitting, on the lumpy armchair in Ginny's office, balancing a cup and saucer in one hand and a plate of biscuits in the other, while he tried to get comfortable. Ginny was pleased to see her old school friend Adam, not just because it gave her an excuse to put aside her bookkeeping, a task she found extremely tedious, but because Ginny valued his friendship. No one knew more than Adam just how difficult she found it to leave the house, in constant fear of suffering a panic attack, and Ginny couldn't express how much she appreciated the help he had given her to battle her anxiety. Whilst she had ventured further afield on a few occasions, it was a journey that was progressing literally one step at a time. More than this, though, she enjoyed Adam's company. In the years that had followed the accidental death of her husband, Roger, she could not have imagined that she would have enjoyed spending time with another man, apart from the clients she represented as a theatrical agent.

'So, what did you want to ask me about?' Then, noticing Adam trying and failing to relax in the armchair, Ginny added, 'You know, we could have gone through to the conservatory.'

'No, it's okay. It has a bearing on what I want to say. Since I came into the orbit of all of you creatives, you and your actors...'

'The Dead Actors,' Ginny interrupted. That was how the four actors, all living in Shepton Rise, affectionately referred to themselves, as they had all been killed off in long-running dramas on TV.

'Yes, well, I've felt inspired to do something creative myself. As you know, I was a travel agent before I lost my wife, Mary, and we used to go on holiday a lot - perks of the job. In those days, I took lots of photos, not just holiday snaps of Mary and our Robbie, but location shots too. I used to like exploring back streets and markets as well as photographing landscapes and beach scenes. Anyway, I put my camera away when Mary died, but now I'd like to resurrect my old hobby. However, I would like to shift the emphasis. I don't just want to take glossy travelogue pictures but documentary photos too.'

'That sounds a marvellous idea,' enthused Ginny.

'I've got an idea about photographing people in their workplaces,' continued Adam, encouraged by Ginny's reaction. 'Especially taking pictures of people who sit at desks, hence the relevance of all this.' Adam indicated Ginny's untidy office with a sweep of the hand. 'Ever since the Covid epidemic, many more people have been working from home. There will be all sorts of different scenarios and backdrops. Sorry, I'm getting carried away now. I'll need some better kit, though. My old thirty-five-millimetre camera won't cut the mustard any more. Not that I would cut mustard with a camera anyway.'

'I think it's a smashing idea, and I know someone you could approach,' said Ginny excitedly, rummaging through the jumble of paperwork on her desk.

'I rather hoped you would,' said Adam sheepishly.

'The editor of "Out and About" is a friend of mine. You know, the glossy magazine we all get delivered free each month. I'm sure I've got a copy here somewhere! I doubt you would receive payment, but the exposure could be valuable. Who knows where it could lead to!'

'Brilliant! Exposure - you're already using photographic lingo. Now, if there's a second cup of tea in the pot, maybe we could move to the conservatory after all.'

2

Late Monday Morning.

Ginny switched on the radio in the kitchen as she washed up the teacups.

"Atlantic systems bring rain from the North and West, with some sun in central areas and light showers in the Southeast. As rain moves off Monday night, skies may clear in places, leading to colder spots."

'That's enough of that!' Ginny said firmly, switching over to Classical Gold FM.

***

After leaving Ginny's house, Adam's quickest

route home was to walk down the High Street, though it was strewn with temptations. The first of these was Heavenly Delights Bakery. He glanced inside to see if there was a queue; there wasn't, so he cheerfully entered the shop. *Still, even if there was a line of people leading out of the shop waiting to be served, which there frequently is, I would have joined them anyway! I fancy one of those honey-dripping flapjacks. Or maybe I should treat myself to a chocolate Florentine biscuit loaded with nuts and candied fruit. I think I owe it to myself to buy one!* Inside, Ashley Lewis, the owner, was staring at the solitary remaining Florentine displayed under the glass counter.

'Morning, Ashley,' greeted Adam cheerfully, 'Oh, I was rather looking forward to one of those, but I wouldn't want to deprive you of it.'

'No, really, have it. You would be doing me a favour. Someone whose name I shan't mention told me I need to lose weight. Tactful, he is not!'

'Apart from the fact that I don't agree with him, I wouldn't dare say such a thing! I'm shocked!'

'Well, power goes to some people's heads.'

Might I ask, was it a certain Mr Lewis?'

'Oh no!' laughed Ashley, 'He's got no power in our house. If he said such a thing, I'd stick his head in the bread oven and turn it to full power. Anything else for you, Adam?'

'Can I have half a dozen of your raspberry honey flapjacks, please? They are our Robbie's favourites. '

'How's he getting on, your Robbie? Is he enjoying being a policeman?' asked Ashley, as she eased the flapjacks into a paper bag.

'Yes, he is. It's kind of you to ask. Of course, it's not easy for him. Robbie finds his Sergeant a bit abrasive; he thinks Robbie is a country bumkin.

'That's not fair! He's a lovely boy. I haven't seen him for ages,' commented Ashley. 'That's five pounds forty pence, please.'

'Thanks. Yes Robbie spends a lot of his time in the city, and, as you'll know, there are some bad things going on there. He has to deal with many weird and unpredictable people. I think he'd prefer to be pedalling a pushbike around a town like Shepton Rise, where nothing really happens, like in the old days of black and white TV.'

'Yeah, but he's got a cushy life with his dad cooking all his meals and buying him biscuits, so it's not all bad! They are rather yummy, those raspberry flapjacks, if I say so myself!' As Adam left, he glanced through the window and noticed Ashley staring at the biscuits on display, lost in her thoughts; then she turned away and swatted viciously at a fly that had dared to enter her domain.

Ashley's got a point, thought Adam as he continued down the High Street, *A cushy life, eh? I'd better think about what I'm going to feed Robbie tonight. I can't give him flapjacks for his dinner. Now, what do I fancy?* Adam gazed through the Prime Cuts butcher's window in fascination. *Dear me! I wouldn't like to get on the wrong side of him!*

Inside, Jack Knight was taking advantage of the fact that there were no customers in the shop and was separating a rack of ribs. What caught Adam's eye was the force the butcher was using. Jack raised the cleaver high in the air and then slammed it down onto the block so hard that it caused the ribs to rise into the air. Adam could see that Jack was uttering something with each blow.

Eventually, Adam entered the shop, trying to time it to a moment just after impact.

'Is it safe to come in, Jack?'

'Sure, don't mind me. Some people get rid of stress by punching a cushion. Me? I take it out on ribs,' laughed Jack. 'I'm alright now; I've calmed down.'

'So what's stressing you out, Jack? Have you been dealing with some tricky customers?'

'Oh, it's never customers,' replied Jack, piling the ribs into a steel bowl and wiping his hands on his bloody apron. 'It's just one individual. Anyway, what can I get you?'

'I didn't know what to buy until I came in, but now I think we'll have ribs tonight. I've got a great recipe. I slow-cook them in the oven, marinated in my homemade barbecue sauce.'

'Sounds delicious, Adam. You certainly won't be grilling them outside on the barbecue until this weather changes! I prepared a trayful of chicken kebabs on skewers this morning. How many have I sold? None! I tell you, whoever's in charge of this bleedin' weather wants shooting.' As Adam left the shop, he heard Jack taking out his frustrations on another rack of ribs. Thump! Thump! Thump!

Adam couldn't remember if he had any apple cider vinegar in his kitchen cupboard, but he was fairly certain he had all the other ingredients for his special barbecue sauce. To save having to come back later, he decided to buy a bottle anyway. *It's a sure way of guaranteeing I'll find another five bottles when I get home,* he laughed to himself. While he could walk further on to the deli, it would be easier to call into QuickMart first. Somehow, QuickMart was holding its own against competition from the big-brand supermarkets. It was helped by the fact that the Council kept turning down plans for other stores to develop sites on the edge of town. However, lately, more and more vans delivering orders from online sites could be seen crawling down the High Street searching for customers' addresses and causing traffic jams by stopping in the middle of the road or else parking half on the pavement so mobility scooters and mothers with pushchairs couldn't get by. There was one such van opposite QuickMart now, delivering to a flat over one of the shops, and it was causing the manager, Matthew Walker, to clench his fists in anger as he peered out of his window.

Whilst Adam wasn't aware of Matthew's seething animosity when he slipped into the shop, Elsie, who was behind the till, was ever mindful of her boss's mood swings and knew she had to tread carefully. Matthew could be charming, but he could also be irritable or sarcastic. Some townsfolk had taken to calling the supermarket Quick Tempered instead of QuickMart, but they still came, because they all loved Elsie.

Fortunately for Elsie, someone else was to bear the brunt of Matthew's anger today. Lenny Peters peeked around the door, failed to see Matthew by the window, and crept into the shop. Lenny used to work at the supermarket as a shelf stacker, but he had fallen asleep in the stockroom after consuming a liquid lunch one day. Matthew had discovered him, sacked him on the spot, and barred him from the shop. Except that Elsie frequently turned a blind eye and served him because she felt sorry for him.

'Out!' thundered Matthew.

'Please, Mr Walker, I just wanted...'

'Out! You're not welcome here!' Matthew grabbed Lenny by the elbow and shoved him out of the door, causing him to stumble and sprawl on the pavement.

Adam approached the counter, clutching a bottle of cider vinegar and feeling uncomfortable. He had witnessed Lenny's forcible expulsion but thought it wasn't his place to comment.

'Hello Matthew,' he said, trying to lighten the atmosphere, 'Have you got one of your theatre productions coming up? I enjoyed the last one.' Matthew switched to the more congenial side of his personality.

'That's very nice of you to say so, Adam. Actually, we have just started rehearsals for a play by Ira Levin called *Deathtrap*. I do hope you will come and see it. I think it's going to be a roaring success.'

'You'll make a killing!' laughed Adam.

'Dr Jekkyll and Mr Hyde might be more appropriate,' muttered Elsie once Matthew was out of earshot.

Adam responded with a wink.

'I don't have any more cash on me; I'll have to use this,' said Adam, pulling out his phone. 'I've only recently started using my phone to pay for things instead of a card. It's a bit new-fangled for me but I want to improve my technology skills.'

'Getting down with the kids!' laughed Elsie. Adam pressed a button and a brightly coloured app launched on his phone. Strawberries, lemons and cherries danced across the screen; then messages zoomed in from infinity.

"Spin & Win. Play now! Click the Spin button, and you can win up to £50 instantly. Prizes of £5, £10, £20, and £50 available all day every day!"

'Oops, not that!' said Adam, feeling flustered. He tried to close the app down, but another one took its place.

"Welcome Offer. Bet £10 on any sports. Get £45 in Free Bets. 18+ New customers only."

'Oh dear, I'm not doing so well here.' Finally,

Adam's bank card was displayed on the screen, and he offered it to the machine on the counter.'

'Thank you,' said Elsie. 'See you, Adam. Be lucky!'

3

Monday Afternoon

"…and the leaders have reached Tattenham Corner, the pivotal halfway point of the Derby here at Epsom Downs. It's still Silent Witness out in front, setting a determined pace, but here comes Red Handed, making a bold move on the outside. Killer Instinct is also gaining ground, inching closer with every stride.

Into the home straight, and it's anyone's race! Silent Witness is trying to hold on, but Deadly Pursuit is closing fast, and now Killer Instinct is launching a powerful surge on the far side!

As they come up to the finish, Red Handed is fading, and it's Deadly Pursuit and Prime Suspect neck and neck! Killer Instinct is not far behind on the near side, giving it everything. Silent Witness is right there, too, charging forward, but it's going to be close!

It's Prime Suspect by a head! Prime Suspect! Prime Suspect is the winner of this year's Derby at Epsom! What an incredible finish!"

Lenny Peters turned away from the TV set and screwed up his betting slip, tossing it to the floor. He stamped on it repeatedly, his frustration and desire for vengeance evident to the other drinkers in The Red Lion, who turned to look at him. Some smiled in amusement; others shook their heads or tutted their disapproval.

'Another pint,' Lenny growled to the landlord, Pete.

'I take it that you didn't win, Lenny,' laughed Pete, pouring a pint of bitter. 'Is that it for today? It's five o'clock now.'

'Nope, I've got the six-thirty at Lingfield to come. I'll have this pint, and then I'll head down to BetMasters.'

'Do you not put your bets on over the phone?'

asked Pete.

'No, I do not! I don't hold with it,' replied Lenny. 'All this interweb betting nonsense is taking the humanity out of the fine art of gambling.' He drained his glass, smacked his lips and belched. 'Ah, that's better!' Lenny turned and tottered out of the pub, almost knocking over Emma as she came through the door to start her evening shift.

'Charming!' she remarked to Pete as she gathered some empty glasses and placed them on the counter.

'Ah, don't mind him, it's just Lenny. His life revolves around drinking and horse racing. He doesn't have time for pleasantries.'

'It doesn't look like either gives him much pleasure,' laughed Emma as she bent down to retrieve Lenny's flattened betting slip.

'Yeah, he can get a bit mean when he's had a few too many, especially after I think he's had enough and won't serve him.'

***

'See you tomorrow, Bert,' said Patrick as he closed the library door behind the last of his regulars and turned the key in the lock. Normally, by now, Bert would be spending much of his time sitting on a park bench, enjoying the sunshine and reading a newspaper or leafing through a murder mystery novel, but not this year. The weather was too cold and unpredictable.

Patrick was working on his own. His assistant had left early to collect her child from the nursery, so it would take him longer than usual to tidy up. He didn't mind. The Library was his second home. Actually, he often thought of it as his first home - he had all he needed here - it was a repository for thousands of years of knowledge, it was warm and light, and he even had a small kitchenette. Often, Patrick didn't feel any need to go home; he could read, and he could dream.

Back in his office, Patrick reread the letter from the Council. As part of a national safeguarding exercise, they were sending a computer expert to check for any improper use of the facilities on library premises.

'Dear, oh dear, oh dear,' he muttered. Patrick did not like any outside interference. He was the master of this domain. Of course, he was the first to agree that one had to protect children, but he was certain that here, there were none of the more unsavoury characters that you would find in the city, so this felt like the Council were just meddling to show they were doing their bit.

Patrick's phone rang; he saw that it was Matthew.

'Hi, Patrick. I just wanted to know what you

thought of the poster for *Deathtrap*. I think it's rather splendid, but I didn't want to go ahead without your approval. After all, you hold the purse strings, and this illustrator is a little more expensive than our previous one, but I think she's worth it.'

'I like it too. It's very striking, and I love the rendition of the typewriter. Very film noir.'

'Good, I'll tell her to take it to the next stage. Actually, we must have a meeting to discuss budgets.'

'Yes, we must, although I'm very busy here at the Library; I've got a book festival coming up.'

'Are you alright? You sound a bit flat.'

'Oh, it's just that the Council are sending someone to inspect the computer system. You know I don't like change.'

'Ah well, I'm sure it will be fine. After all, this is Shepton Rise! See you soon. Bye, Patrick.'

***

Lenny walked into BetMasters. Visiting the Bookies didn't give him the same pleasure that he used to get from it in the old days. There was nothing to beat stepping in from a cold, rainy day to the warm, embracing, smokey fug of a betting shop. The soundtrack of a horse race in progress, broadcast from a black and white television delivered by maestros like Peter O'Sullevan or Richard Hoiles. Pure poetry! *What was that poem we did at school? wondered Lenny, It was about a night train. I liked that one. It chugged along just like being on a train. When you heard Peter O'Sullevan in full flow, it was just like that. You felt the beat of the hooves, the snort of the horses and the roar of the crowd all wrapped up in the sound of his voice. And now, what have we got?* Lenny looked around with distaste. Outside, the town planners had forced BetMasters' shop designers to curb their enthusiasm and tone down their ideas to suit the nature of a High Street shop in a conservation area, but it didn't stop them from going to town inside. *There are so many bright lights and so much colour that it's like being in a playground. Obviously, there's no smoking, but there's even a plug-in air freshener, for goodness sake! And the things people bet on these days! What happened to the sport of kings? Nowadays, people bet on whether some overpaid footballer will fall on his bum within the first five minutes of a game! Or if a budgie will perch on the net at Wimbledon! Ah well, I'll just have to put up with it because I have a good feeling about the six-thirty at Lingfield.*

'Hello Lenny,' smiled Dawn from behind the glass screen, 'Are you feeling lucky?'

'I always feel lucky. But being it and feeling it are two different things,'

'You're not wrong,' laughed Dawn. Even if she wasn't working in a betting shop, she would never gamble herself. It was all too obvious which way the money flowed. With a few exceptions, it streamed from the punters via her cash desk into BetMasters' tills. She didn't complain; it paid her wages. 'It looks like you could do with a patch on your tweed jacket there, Lenny. You've had that for a long time.'

'Agh!' Lenny inspected the elbow of his jacket. 'It was that...that...I wouldn't dream of saying the word in my head in your company, Dawn, but it was that Matthew Walker. He threw me out of his shop for no good reason, and it ripped. I'll tell you, one of these days...'

***

Five players are in the game. The dealer is prettier than the girl last night. DON'T GET DISTRACTED. She deals two cards to each player and two to herself. What have I got? An ace and a five. OH NO! WHY ME? WHEN WILL I GET A DECENT HAND? I can see she's got a Queen, and the other is still face down. I've no choice; I click "Hit" PLEASE, A FIVE OR A SIX. YES! A SIX! I click Stand, as do players two and three. Player four has got some guts - selected Double Down and received another card. Hah! That's not what you want when you've just doubled your stakes - a nine. You are bust, my friend. Player five is sitting pretty with a blackjack. The dealer reaches to turn her card. PLEASE NOT AN ACE, PLEASE NOT AN ACE. It's an eight! We all won, except, of course, for player four, who went bust. I'm still down overall, but this is the start of a winning streak. Let's play!

4

Tuesday

'Hello, are you the Landlord?'

Business was slow, so Pete was leaning on the counter reading a newspaper. He straightened up to see a lady, who he guessed to be in her forties, wearing a white linen shirt with the collar turned up and a cashmere cardigan.

'Yes, I am, love.'

'Hello, my name's Susan Cunningham-Hill. I'm with a whole load of chums, and I was wondering if you might be showing the tennis match that's about to start. We could go to our tennis club and watch it, but we thought it might make a change to watch it here. I presume you've got plenty of gin and tonic?'

Pete glanced up at the TV; an episode of Murder She Wrote was broadcasting to an empty room.

'By all means, I'll turn it over. Sorry, Angela,' he called to the actress on the screen, 'I can't wait to the end; I reckon it was the jealous lover who did it, anyway. And to answer your question, love, we've gallons of gin and tonic.'

'Jolly good! I'll go and get the girls. They are in the queue at Heavenly Delights.'

After Susan Cunningham-Hill had left the pub, Pete took out his phone and rang his barmaid, Emma. Her shift was due to start shortly.

'Pop into QuickMart and buy a box of tonic water on your way in, love. I don't want to run out.'

An hour later, the pub had livened up. It wasn't just the ladies from the tennis club who were in; many regulars had arrived, too.

"15 - love

30 - love

30 -15"

'Oy!' shouted Lenny in the general direction of the

bar, 'I want the other side on. My horse is running at Sandown. I've had a tip and I want to see her romp home.' Emma looked at Pete with alarm; she wasn't sure how she should handle the situation. Susan Cunningham-Hill and her friends were cheering on the tennis match. Pete had needed to break into the box of tonic water Emma had bought, which was a sign that the gin was flowing freely. Until Lenny's interjection, the atmosphere was perfect. It was just how a traditional English pub should be.

Pete stepped in.

'Sorry, Lenny, we have had customers watching the tennis since before you came in.'

'They've had it on for ages. 's not fair! It's my turn now.' Lenny was becoming belligerent. His slurred speech indicated that he had been drinking all day.

'Sorry, Lenny, it doesn't work like that. They want to watch the whole game, set and match. It will be Wimbledon next month, so this is an important warm-up competition,' replied Pete.

'Hah! 's rubbish!' Lenny scoffed. He drained the rest of his beer, then angrily threw the empty glass to the floor. Everyone in the pub turned at the sound of the smashing glass. A cheer and laughter came from customers in the snug who couldn't see this ugly scene and presumed someone had accidentally dropped their glass. Pete, however, was not amused. He strode forward, grabbed Lenny by the shoulders, and marched him towards the door. In his younger days, Lenny had been quite a useful Bantamweight boxer, but years of drinking and poor diet had robbed him of the ability he once had, and he was no match for Pete.

'That's it. I've had enough! You're barred,' Pete said firmly and deposited Lenny on the street before shouting, 'Go home, Lenny and sober up!'

Forty minutes later, the change of atmosphere in the pub was remarkable. Emma had swept up the broken glass. The tennis match had finished, but the ladies who had been watching it were exuberant after the young English girl had fought back to win her first major championship and, having been treated to a round of free drinks by Pete to make up for the disturbance caused by Lenny, they were already making plans to return to the Red Lion to watch Wimbledon.

'I'll put on some nosh if you like,' offered Pete cheerfully.

'Strawberries and cucumber sandwiches?' suggested one of the ladies.

'I was thinking pork pies and sausage rolls,' replied Pete with a laugh.

He turned to watch the weather forecast on TV.

"Tuesday brings rain to Northern Ireland and Western Scotland, while southern and western areas stay mostly dry with some sun. The Midlands turn windier with more rain. Warmer in the south, cooler elsewhere."

'I hope the weather improves in time for Wimbledon,' Pete commented. 'Never mind winning a Grand Slam; they'll just be making a grand splash in a giant puddle at this rate! I'll turn this off - too depressing - and put some music on.' Pete pressed a button to start his playlist. The first chords pounded out. It was the Weather Girls - "It's Raining Men". 'Now that can only be a good thing!' announced Pete cheerfully. Emma rolled her eyes - she had heard Pete say this once too often!

The ladies left, chuckling, and shaking their heads in amusement. They were soon followed by the drinkers in the snug, but no sooner had Pete wiped down the tables and returned the empty glasses to the bar than Julia, Angie, and Doc arrived. It was a Tuesday, the evening the Dead Actors always met.

'Ooh, your fringe is a lovely shade of pink,' commented Emma.

'Isn't it just,' Angie replied, 'It said on the bottle that it's fuchsia, but I would say it's more Barbie.'

'It matches your earrings.' Angie turned her head so Emma could see her other ear. 'Oops, I was wrong. That one's yellow.' Laughing, Angie picked up the glass of wine that Pete had already poured for her and joined the others in the snug.

'I always love it when Angie comes in. You never know what colour her hair will be,' said Emma.

'Yeah!' replied Pete, 'She explained it to me once. She said that during all those years of acting in soaps, the one thing she could never do was change her hair. And it was never outlandish because she always played ordinary roles, like working in the cafe, or the shop, or...as a barmaid.'

'Cheek! Ordinary! You watch, I'll come with a bright green Mohican tomorrow!'

Pete was still chuckling when Steve arrived.

'I suppose I'm last as usual,' said Steve. Pete nodded. 'I'll pick up the tab then. It usually evens out by the end of the night.'

A short time later, Adam popped his head around the snug door, clutching a pint of bitter.

'Mind if I join you?'

'Sure, pull up a chair,' said Steve. 'How's Ginny? Is she coming?'

'She's fine. A bit snowed under trying to catch up

with the accounts,' replied Adam.

'It wouldn't surprise me if it started to snow; this weather's been appalling for June,' Angie chipped in.

'So no, she's not coming tonight,' continued Adam. 'She's been taking it steadily. She's still uncomfortable leaving the house, but we've had a few coffees at the garden centre cafe, and I'm going with her to visit the accountants. So, making progress.'

'I've got some news,' announced Angie, 'Ricky Flynn's house purchase has gone through, so he'll be moving in. I'm not sure how much time he will spend here though, as he's keeping his apartment in London.'

'So does that mean he will officially become one of the Dead Actors?' asked Adam.

'Hmmm!' mused Doc, 'We've all been killed off on TV, and he hasn't, so he's more one of the Living Dead.'

'Like a zombie,' suggested Steve, 'Hey, do you know why zombies don't eat comedians?'

'Go on,' sighed Julia.

'Because they taste funny!' Steve laughed. Everyone else groaned. 'Seriously though, the scrapes he gets into, I wonder how he hasn't ended up in an early grave!'

'I've got some news too,' announced Julia, 'Do you

remember that we all went along to see that Stage Centre production last year?'

'Yes, you mean *What the Butler Saw?* The local am-dram group?' Angie recalled.

Julia nodded. 'That's them. I've been asked to help out as assistant director.'

'I know the guys in charge,' said Adam, 'Patrick handles the business side of things. He works in the library. And Matthew runs the creative side of the operation. He's the manager at QuickMart.'

'It was Mathew that contacted me,' said Julia.

'He can be a little temperamental,' continued Adam, 'He can rub people up the wrong way.'

'Reading between the lines, I have the feeling that is why he got in touch with me. He wants someone to smooth things out between him and the actors.'

'Smoothing is one thing you are definitely good at,' commented Angie. 'I've never seen you come out wearing anything that needed ironing.'

'I can tell you one thing,' said Julia, stroking the arm of her Armani jacket, a charity shop find from Kensington, 'I may have no choice about growing old, but I shall never grow old and wrinkled.'

'Botox?' suggested Doc.

'No dear. I'll stay away from cheap gin, which

reminds me, it's your round.'

5

Sunday

Ricky Flynn, the infamous and slightly inebriated actor, had arrived at his new house on Saturday evening with his latest girlfriend and two bottles of champagne packed in his suitcase, but the romantic evening had not gone well.

'Where on earth are we?' she had asked, 'Shepton Rise is in the middle of bleedin' nowhere. I bet there ain't even a sushi bar or a nightclub! And where's your furniture? There ain't nuffing here! You can bleedin' well take me back to the station. I'm catching the first train back to London. You stay here if you want, but I ain't stayin' wiv you. I wanna get back to civilisation.'

Ricky had just shrugged in response. It was a definite probability that the citizens of Shepton Rise were more civilised than she was, but he couldn't be bothered to argue.

After putting his soon-to-be ex-girlfriend on a train, Ricky called in for a beer at the Railway Inn. After that, he returned to his new home and spent the rest of the night watching videos on his phone and drinking champagne straight from the bottle, as there were no glasses in the house. There was no bed either. Eventually, he fell asleep lying on the bedroom carpet.

Early on Sunday morning, Ricky woke, stretched his aching limbs and decided to go in search of either a cafe or a shop selling food. He stopped at QuickMart but saw the door was closed and the shop was in darkness. Then he noticed a sign that said it didn't open until ten o'clock on a Sunday. As he turned to walk on, Ricky saw a pair of legs sticking out from behind the bins of QuickMart's service area. He was curious and went to investigate. The recumbent figure of a man, many years Ricky's senior, was lying half inside a metal cage of the type which delivery men used to wheel in boxes of supermarket supplies. Ricky had a strange feeling of kinship with the snoring man. This was partly because he had spent a similarly uncomfortable night on his floor, albeit numbed by champagne, but also because Ricky was reminded of a moment in his life. A young girl had found him slumped on a London pavement and, having recognised him and checked his key fob, had got him back to his hotel before the paparazzi could find him. Ricky didn't know her name or even whether she had stayed the night as she had vanished by the morning. But here was an opportunity for payback.

'It's karma, man,' he muttered as he reached down and shook the snoring figure. 'Hey, man! How about we get some breakfast?'

Lenny sat up, blinking, trying to rouse himself. Then Ricky noticed that Lenny was clutching a copy of the Racing Post. 'It's a sign, man!' he exclaimed because a headline on the front cover announced: *The Winning Full English: a survey of the best breakfasts available at English racecourses.* 'So, you are a racing man, are you?'

'Oh yes, Sir,' replied Lenny, sleepily.

'Let me look.' Ricky reached for the newspaper and turned to the article about breakfasts. 'Ah, that's quite near here!' he exclaimed. 'Wait here, I'll get a taxi.' Ricky didn't know any local taxi firms and his phone had died the previous night, so he couldn't ring one anyway. However, he knew the way back to the train station and imagined he would find a taxi there. Meanwhile, Lenny had no problem waiting; he closed his eyes and fell asleep again.

Around twenty minutes later, a taxi pulled up outside QuickMart and Ricky leapt out, only to find that Lenny had gone. He knew that he had only passed one couple walking down the high street, so he got back in the taxi and instructed the driver to drive on. He spied his quarry slumped on a low garden wall. The taxi pulled alongside him, and Ricky opened the door.

'Come on, man. We're going for breakfast!' Lenny was still more than half drunk from the night before and had decided the earlier encounter with this stranger had been a dream. He tottered over and half fell into the taxi. Ten minutes later, Frank, the taxi driver, smiled as he glanced in his mirror because both of his passengers were fast asleep. This would be a nice, quiet ride. He had negotiated a generous fixed price for the journey, and the cash was already nestled in his pocket.

Frank listened with interest to the weather forecast.

"A significant low-pressure system will bring a windy Monday with extensive cloud cover and widespread rain, especially in the North and West. By Thursday, the low-pressure

system will dominate the whole country, resulting in strong winds and heavy rain."

Frank smiled. He didn't mind at all. This was his last shift and that evening he and his wife would be flying out to Spain for a fortnight's holiday in search of some summer sun. He would toast the lousy English weather with a glass of sangria over a bowl of paella.

'That was certainly a tasty breakfast,' said Lenny, smacking his lips, 'And this orange juice is very refreshing. Can we get a couple more?'

'An excellent idea, my friend,' replied Ricky, gesturing to the waitress. 'Can we have two more glasses of Bucks Fizz, he said, smiling sweetly, 'No, I'll tell you what, you may as well bring two each. They are going down rather well.' As the waitress piled the breakfast plates onto her tray and balanced the six empty glasses on it, she couldn't quite place where she had seen the younger man before. They were an odd couple; one was wearing a black, fringed and embroidered suede jacket, his long hair worn in a plait. She wasn't to know that Ricky was growing his hair for a forthcoming pirate film. His companion was a diminutive man wearing a tatty tweed jacket with a rip on the elbow and a flat cap. She returned with the drinks and then thought no more about it. A long and busy day stretched ahead - no time for daydreams!

'Here we are then,' said Ricky, handing Lenny one of the race day programmes he had bought. 'What do you fancy for the first race?

'Well, now, I'll have to study this. With all the rain we've been having, the going will be heavy to soft. Let's have a look at the horses in the Parade Ring. I'll show you how to pick out a winner.'

Ten minutes later, Ricky and Lenny watched the jockeys lead their horses around the ring prior to the first race.'

'Now look at number four; see how sleek and shiny his coat is,' commented Lenny, 'And look at that powerful back end. Rippling with muscles. That's going to be important on this soft ground.' Lenny glanced back at his programme, jabbing his finger on it. 'He's called *Deadly Revenge*. Look at those stats. My money's on four, or it would be if I had any left.'

'Ah! Don't worry about that, my friend. I can sub you - pay me back out of your winnings. I fancy number nine,' said Ricky.

'Why would you pick her? She looks really nervous.'

'I like the name, *Standing Ovation*, I'm an actor, you see.'

'That's a daft way of picking a horse. Come on, let's put a bet on.'

A few hours later, Ricky was laughing at Lenny's expense as he queued up at the on-course bookmakers to collect his winnings, for the third time that day. 'You're really having an unlucky day' chuckled Ricky. 'I thought you had a winner there, but my horse, *Oscar's Delight*, pipped you at the post.'

'I should have backed it each way,' grumbled Lenny, 'Only I backed it to win.'

'Come on, old pal, I think it's time for a plate of sandwiches and a nice bottle of Sauvignon next. I tell you what,' said Ricky, stuffing some money and a betting slip into Lenny's top pocket, 'You can have my Tote ticket. It might bring you luck. The first three horses on the accumulator have romped home.' Lenny nodded absently to acknowledge the gift but was preoccupied with trying to puzzle out why his surefire certain winners were performing so poorly.

Lenny's luck didn't improve throughout the rest of the afternoon. He didn't pick a single horse that finished in the first three places. Strangely for him, he didn't get disgruntled and angry. The presence of his ebullient companion, plus the endless supply of alcohol, meant that by the end of the day, he was laughing just as hard as Ricky about his misfortune.

Later, as the taxi driver looked in his mirror to see both men fast asleep, just as Frank had done that morning, he felt pleased to have been flagged down by this odd couple. A quiet drive, with enough cash in his pocket to cover the long journey home back through two counties, was an excellent way to finish the day.

When he pulled into Shepton Rise, he called to wake his two passengers and ask for directions.

'This will do me. Just pull up here; you've just passed the end of my road,' slurred the older man. As Lenny rolled out of the taxi, Ricky called to him.

'I'll be seeing you, Lucky Jim.'

'Ha ha,' laughed Lenny as he staggered off into the night.

'Carry on to the station,' sang out Ricky to the driver, 'Hopefully, I can catch a train to London tonight.'

6

Sunday Evening

'Hi Matthew. Are you there? You are cutting it a bit fine. I'm still at the Library. Ring me back.'

***

The only company Ginny needed tonight was Tuxie. A cat wouldn't drag you off into the future, eagerly seeking out excitement and adventure in the way that a dog would. No, with a cat on your lap, you had time to journey back into your memories and try to make sense of your life. Adam had looked disappointed when she turned down his offer to bring a home-cooked meal round.

'Oh, that does sound lovely, Adam, but can we do it on another night? I really can't relax until I've made some headway with these accounts.' But that was an excuse. Ginny had no intention of going anywhere near her accounts - not tonight.

Her phone pinged; it was an alert from Facebook. *Bradley commented on a post you are following in Roger Fellows.* Neither Ginny nor her husband, Roger, had been prolific social media users. Maybe it would have been different if they had had children, but that never worked out for them. It wasn't a conscious decision - it just never happened. They were both only children and couldn't help feeling a sense of guilty relief when friends who had arrived to visit with a boisterous brood had finally left. It was one of those friends, now divorced, who had left the message.

'Hey, mate. Have a happy birthday up there in Heaven. Hope the angels throw a good party. Thinking of you!'

I wonder how long these accounts will stay live? wondered Ginny. Not that she knew how to close an account down or if it was even possible. *If Facebook still exists in a hundred years, will Roger's account continue to send out birthday reminders to people who have passed away? Perhaps it's feasible to schedule a message to be sent automatically every year far into the future!*

For now, though, it was time for contemplation, to stroke Tuxie, and to toast Roger's memory with a glass of Chardonnay.

***

Shepton Rise is not unique in having a historic Corn Exchange building dating back to the 1840s. Like others across the country, it is no longer a hub where farmers and merchants gather to discuss the price of wheat and barley. Fortunately, in the 1960s, the Town Council chose to preserve the building rather than demolish it, transforming it into a valuable community asset.

Today, the Corny is bustling with activity. Youth clubs and art groups use its rooms and several times a week dance classes are held there, inspiring the next Ginger Rogers, Darcey Bussell, or Beyoncé to dream of a life in the spotlight. Before the rise of digital streaming, a movie club called Pop Corny met there, showing films once a month. Moviegoers were easily recognisable, usually to be seen carrying a cushion and a bottle of wine.

In common with many of Britain's Corn

Exchanges, the Corny also served as a theatre venue. Apart from the various Tribute Acts that strutted their stuff on stage, the occasional professional touring theatre company, and, of course, the Pantomime, it was also home to the local amateur dramatic group, Stage Centre. Julia was a little apprehensive about her first directorial outing, but as she walked into the rehearsal room, she was careful not to let it show.

'Hello,' she said, offering her hand to the first person she saw, 'My name's Julia. Did Matthew tell you all that I was coming tonight? We have met before in your flower shop.'

'Oh, yes. I'm Samantha. I've been looking forward to meeting you. I remember you in *Stirling Heights*. I can remember your fall to your death so vividly.'

'It was very realistic, wasn't it? I hope you weren't mentally scarred by it! It was less dramatic for me - I was just suspended in front of a green screen, waving my arms and legs around! The CGI team did the rest.'

'We've met too. I'm Jack from Prime Cuts, and no, we still don't have any vegan sausages!'

Julia laughed. 'That was for my son, Rupert. It was just a phase. This week, he has decided he is gluten-free. I'm pleased to meet you, Jack. And of course I've met you too, Ashley. Is there anyone in

Shepton Rise who hasn't bought a cake from Heavenly Delights?'

'You'd be surprised,' replied Ashley, 'Those on a budget get seduced by Matthew's range of cheapo cakes. His basics range.'

'Yeah, but they basically taste like cardboard! Hello, Julia. I'm Chris - I do all the lighting and sound and stuff.'

'Thanks for giving up your Sunday evening, Julia,' said Samantha.

'That's okay, I've got spare time at the moment. I'm between jobs. Anyway, it's a bank holiday tomorrow. Are Patrick and Matthew coming tonight?'

'I doubt if Patrick will come,' replied Ashley 'He doesn't get involved at this stage. He deals with the financial side of things. Matthew's usually here by now, though,' replied Ashley. Just then, Chris's phone rang.

'Talk of the devil, well, one of them anyway. Here's Patrick now,' said Chris, glancing at the screen. 'Hello. No, he's not here.' Chris listened for a few moments, then put the phone in his pocket. 'Patrick's looking for Matthew too. Matthew and him were supposed to have a meeting earlier, but our esteemed director didn't turn up.'

'Can I suggest we make a start,' said Julia quickly,

sensing a little tension in the atmosphere. 'I am already familiar with *Deathtrap* because I saw it on Broadway.'

'Oh, lucky you!' gasped Ashley.

'Yes, we were doing a few location shots in New York for *Stirling Heights* as, fortunately for me, there were scenes the TV company couldn't mock up in the studio. I had some spare time because it rained, so I managed to catch a few shows. Anyway, let's run down the cast list. We've got five characters. So, who plays Sidney Bruhl, the playwright?'

Jack raised a hand, 'That's me.'

'And I'm his wife, Myra,' added Samantha.

'So, are you Helga, the psychic?' Julia asked Ashley, receiving a nod. 'What about the student, Clifford Anderson?'

'Ah, he actually is a student - Jay. He's got exams at the moment. He will be here next week,' replied Jack.

'And that leaves Porter, the attorney. Is that you, Chris?'

'No, it flaming well, isn't,' retorted Chris bitterly. I'm going to get on with wiring these lights.' Chris stamped off to the other side of the hall and rooted noisily in his toolbox.

'I'm afraid you've hit a sore spot there,' whispered Samantha, 'You see, Matthew and he had a big argument about it. Chris wants to act in our plays, but Matthew never lets him. Matthew is an actor-director. He's playing the role of Porter.'

'Ah! The elusive Matthew Walker,' said Julia. Okay, what I would like to do is to chat with you individually. I'll talk to Chris first, so can the three of you please read through some scenes together; then I'll join in later and stand in for Jay. And Porter, too, if Matthew doesn't turn up.'

Chris had calmed down after his outburst.

'I'm sorry about that,' he said, 'Sometimes that man makes my blood boil.'

'That's fine,' said Julia, soothingly, 'I've come across Matthew in the supermarket, of course, but I don't really know him. He sounds a wee bit, erm, controlling.'

'He blows hot and cold. He's as nice as pie when he wants something, like when he wants me to go in and have a look at the CCTV at the supermarket because it's stopped working, but then when I broach the subject of acting, it's a different story. I know he wants me to work behind the scenes because he hasn't got anyone else to do it, but being an electrician is my day job. I joined the society to have a change from all that. Sometimes, I'd like to fix wires to two bulldog clips. I shan't tell you where I would attach them. Then I would turn on my electric generator to full power!'

'Ouch,' Julia winced, 'That sounds lethal!'

Julia left Chris grumbling to himself as he stripped down a faulty light, and went over to chat with Samantha.

'Has Chris calmed down a bit?' asked Samantha, 'Sometimes Matthew drives people to their limit. He can be infuriating.'

'Do you get on with him?' asked Julia. Samantha's face clouded over. She paused, and Julia looked away, embarrassed.

'I'm sorry,' continued Samantha, 'I was just having a moment. Look, I may as well tell you because the others all know already, that once upon a time, we had a thing going. It was when I was new to the group, and I really thought it was going somewhere. Then stuff happened, I'll spare you the details, and we ended the relationship. When I think back on it, I sometimes feel sad, but mostly I'm incredibly angry. I know that walking away from *Stage Centre* is an option, but I just love being on stage.'

'Are you able to channel those emotions into your performances?'

'That's exactly what I do,' laughed Samantha, 'It's

not always appropriate though. I reckon Matthew thinks I'm suffering from nerves when I'm tense, but I'm not. I'm just furious with him! Ashley's better at hiding her feelings but that's because she's a better actress than I am.'

'I would describe him as inconsiderate and insensitive,' said Ashley later. 'Don't get me wrong, he's a good director, but he can be a bit inflexible. You know - my way or the highway.'

'So, have these character traits impacted you?' enquired Julia.

'Well, there was one time...' Ashley stopped, then changed the subject. 'No, we are here to talk about the play.'

'Okay, so how do you see the part of Helga?' asked Julia.

'It's not how I see it that counts. It's how Matthew sees it. I imagine he wants me to be a cranky old lady as usual.'

'You normally play character roles then?'

'God forbid he should ever make me the leading lady! When the day of reckoning comes, I hope he will be made to pay for all the cutting things he has said.'

When it was Jack's turn to talk to Julia, Ashley went to freshen up.

'While Ashley is out of the room, let me tell you about her and Matthew,' said Jack. 'I doubt she will say this to you herself, but on more than one occasion, Matthew called her fatty in public. He has an image in his head of what a leading lady should look like, and he's made it clear that her body shape doesn't fit the bill, despite the fact that she's a brilliant actor and has a smashing voice.'

'I'm intrigued to get to know this man,' said Julia. 'How do you get on with him?

'My honest opinion? Day to day, face to face, we scrape by - usually - but behind the scenes, I think he can be a bit sly. He doesn't know how much I know.'

'What do you mean?' asked Julia, curious about the man she would have to work with.

'Well, that's for me to know and you to find out,' replied Jack brusquely.

Julia realised it would be unwise to press him further on this and instead gathered all the actors together.

'I think we can assume Matthew isn't coming, so let's crack on with some improvisation games,' she announced. She hoped the group dynamic might make for a more constructive atmosphere; individually, there was too much pent-up anger.

7

Monday Week Two

'Matthew. Why are you playing so hard to get? Ring me when you can. I knocked at your house this morning, but obviously, you weren't in. There was nowhere to park outside QuickMart, so I didn't stop, but I could see it was in darkness. Where are you?'

***

With trembling fingers, Elsie pressed nine nine nine on her phone.

'Emergency. Which service do you require? Fire,

police, or ambulance?'

'Police. Someone has killed my boss, Matthew Walker. He's stone-cold dead!'

Thirty minutes later, the police had cordoned the shop off with blue and white plastic tape, and the forensic team was hard at work recording the murder scene. Detective Sergeant Bristow, annoyed at being dragged over to a backwater like Shepton Rise entered the shop with Detective Constable Robbie Broome.

'I'm not too hopeful here, Sarge,' said the aptly-nicknamed Dusty, who was checking the murder weapon for prints. 'It's a carving knife from the store's kitchen section. It's still got the label attached. So, any number of innocent people could have handled it previously.'

'Now, Broome, I don't want you getting ahead of yourself,' warned Bristow, jabbing a finger at Robbie, 'Just because you are no longer a PC and are now a DC, remember - I'm in charge. Leave the questions to me.' Robbie nodded. His work on solving the murder of Simon Glenn a few months ago had helped him secure promotion, a fact that still rankled with Bristow.

Elsie was waiting in the office, nursing a cup of tea. She appeared pretty calm now.

'Good morning, Mrs Godwin. My name is

Detective Sergeant Bristow, and this is Detective Constable Broome.'

'Hello, Robbie. Nice to see you again. How's your dad? How were your barbecued spare ribs the other day?'

'He's very well, Elsie. And the ribs were delicious.' Robbie could easily have continued to chat; after all, he had known Elsie since he was a schoolboy, queuing up to buy sweets, but he was very aware that Bristow was scowling at him. One thing his boss was not was a neighbourhood policeman!

'Let's get on with it,' growled Bristow. 'Tell us in your own words what happened, and then we will help you prepare a statement.'

'I came in to work at the same time as usual...'

'When was that, Elsie?' asked Robbie.

'Because it's a Bank Holiday, we were opening our normal Sunday hours, from ten to four, so I didn't need to come in until ten minutes before ten o'clock. Matthew always opened the shop and got everything ready half an hour ahead of me.'

'And was the door unlocked this morning?' asked Robbie.

'I think it would be less confusing for Mrs Godwin if I asked all the questions,' interrupted Bristow, clearly irritated.

Elsie managed a wink in Robbie's direction without Bristow seeing.

'Now then, Mrs Godwin, was the door unlocked this morning when you arrived?'

'Yes, just as usual, only the lights were off, which isn't normal.'

'I see, and did you turn them on when you arrived?' pressed Bristow.

'I just flicked the switch by the door, which turns on the lamp over the entrance; the rest of the lights are controlled back here in this office. I didn't need any more light - there was enough for me to see Matthew and to see that he was dead as a doornail. His eyes were wide open, and there was blood everywhere. So I left the shop and rang nine nine nine.'

'When was the last time you saw Matthew Walker?'

'It was on Saturday night. I had Sunday off so we went to the seaside after I finished work on Saturday. We booked it ages ago. I wish we hadn't bothered - we didn't expect it to be so cold. I mean, it's June, for goodness sake!'

'So, when did you return to Shepton Rise, Mrs Godwin?' asked Bristow with exaggerated patience.

'This morning. We set off at the crack of dawn so

I could get here in time for work. We had to miss our cooked breakfast, but the landlady made us up a bag with a selection of pastries and some fruit, and we picked up a cup of tea from a machine in a garage on the way back. I wish I hadn't bothered with that, either. It tasted revolting! I tell you, I was very pleased to be back in Shepton Rise. And then this happened!'

'Presumably, Matthew would cash up at the end of the day,' said Robbie.

'I was just going to ask that, Detective Constable,' snapped Bristow, emphasising the word Constable. Elsie answered without waiting for Bristow to repeat the question.

'That's right. Actually, the odd thing I noticed is that the till is open. All the notes have gone, but the change is still there. I could see that without touching anything, mind. Matthew always cashed up at the end of the day. He would bag up all the coins and put them in the safe along with any paper money. Then, in the morning, He would put a float in the till. You know - a selection of notes and coins so we can give customers change.'

'I know what a float is,' said Bristow, irritably 'Where is the safe?'

'It's right behind you.'

'Do you know the code to open it?'

Elsie looked worried. 'Yes,' she replied slowly, 'But Matthew said I shouldn't tell anyone. Only me, him and the Branch Manager know it.'

'Might I suggest that Mr Walker is not in a position to object,' snapped Bristow. 'Write it on this piece of paper. After the team has dusted the safe for prints, I want to check if the murderer has robbed it. I guarantee that we won't reveal the number to anyone. In any case, your Branch Manager can change the combination.' Elsie duly wrote down the number.

'This may just be a robbery that went wrong, but do you know if Mr Walker had any enemies? Anyone with a grudge against him?' asked Bristow.

'Well, he was a bit Marmite.'

'How do you mean?'

'You know, the spread you have on toast,' replied Elsie.

'I know what Marmite is!'

'Some people love it and others hate it,' continued Elsie, 'He could rub people up the wrong way one moment and then be all sweetness and light the next. But I don't know anyone who disliked him enough to want to murder him.'

'Did anything unusual happen on Saturday, Elsie?'

asked Robbie. Bristow snapped his head around to glower at Robbie, which didn't go unnoticed by Elsie.

'It was all pretty much like it usually is. However, we did manage to run out of Bakewell Tarts, which surprised me because they are not a patch on the ones that Heavenly Delights sells. Ours taste like cardboard! Oh, and there was the confrontation with Lenny.'

'What?' demanded Bristow, ignoring the pastry diversion. 'What confrontation? Who's Lenny?'

'Lenny is one of the locals, Sarge,' explained Robbie. 'He drinks too much and loses all his money on horses.'

'That's right,' continued Elsie. 'Officially, he's barred from the shop, although he tries his luck now and then. Mathew quite literally threw him out of the shop on Saturday. They had a few words. No love lost there!'

'And did anybody else witness this altercation?' asked Bristow.

'Why, yes,' said Elsie, turning to Robbie. 'Your dad was here. It was when he was buying the ingredients for his barbecue sauce. You'll have to tell him to give me the recipe.' Robbie opened his mouth to reply but then, feeling the wave of animosity emanating from Bristow, thought better of it and clamped his lips together. Robbie intercepted another covert wink from Elsie. *She's enjoying winding up the Sarge,* he thought; she's not as daft as she acts!

'I think that will be all for the moment, Mrs Godwin. You can give your contact details to the Detective Constable in case we need to ask you to come down to the station.' Again, Bristow emphasised the word *Constable*. He was definitely too disgruntled to refer to Robbie as a colleague. 'I'm going to check on how the forensic team are getting on.' Much to Bristow's annoyance, as he left the room, he was sure he heard the words *barbecue sauce* in the conversation between his subordinate and Elsie Godwin.

***

Back at the City South Police Station, Detective Sergeant Bristow was feeling quite pleased with himself.

'I think I've done all right there. I wrapped that one up pretty quickly.'He turned to Robbie, who was typing at a nearby desk and barked, 'Have you finished that report yet? I want to read it before I go down to the canteen.'

'Nearly, Sir,' replied Robbie. I just wanted to check with you how much money Lenny left on his bedside table.'

'One hundred and twenty pounds, all in twenty-pound notes. I'd like to see him explain that one away.'

'Thanks, Boss. It's not looking so good for him, is it? I must say, I am surprised. I wouldn't have expected this of Lenny,' said Robbie, frowning.

'When you've been in the Force as long as I have, you'll learn to expect the unexpected,' said Bristow in a patronising tone. 'He hasn't given us an explanation for one single thing yet. Saying that he can't remember what happened yesterday is hardly going to wash in court!'

PC Laura Treadmore poked her head around the door.

'Sarge, that prisoner in the cells, Lenny Peters, is making a fearful racket. He says he's remembered what he did yesterday. He wants to make a statement.'

'Does he now? Has he sobered up?' asked Bristow.

'The duty doctor thinks he is sober enough to be interviewed.'

'Then we'll be only too happy to oblige. Have him brought up to Interview Room One, Treadwell.'

'Yes, Sir,' replied Laura, wondering when the DS would get her name right.

***

For a moment, Lenny was silent, distracted by Robbie, who had started the recording. Lenny was trying to digest the seriousness of the situation. He had been in trouble with the police before, mostly for being drunk and incapable or, occasionally, drunk and disorderly. These offences usually resulted in him spending a night in the cells to sober up and then being released the following day with nothing more than a police caution. He had never ended up in an interview room like this before.

'Whilst you have the right to remain silent, can I remind you that it was you who requested that you talk to us?' said Bristow impatiently. 'You say you have had a revelation and miraculously remembered your whereabouts on Sunday.'

'With respect,' said Price, the duty solicitor, 'Might I suggest that my client would be more forthcoming if you didn't take such a confrontational tone.'

'Well?' said Bristow, ignoring the solicitor, leaning forward and staring Lenny full in the eye.

'Ah yes, you see, I was pondering who was running at Chepstow today when it came to me. I was at the races yesterday,'

'Interesting. And which races were those?'

'You know, Gee-Gees. Horse races.'

'I know what the races are, but where?'

'Ah, I don't really know. I'll have a little think.'

'But surely you must know which racecourse!'

'No, you see, I had a little snooze. In fact, we both did, and when we woke up, we were there.'

'You said we. Did you go with one of your pals?'

'No, Sir. I had never seen him before.'

'Seen who? What was his name.'

'I don't know his name. I didn't think to ask. It didn't seem to matter. Wait a minute! I think he said he was an actor.'

'So, you spent the day at the races but don't know where you were, and with someone you can't remember. Very helpful!' said Bristow sarcastically.

'How was your luck, Lenny?' asked Robbie.

Ah! rotten! I didn't back a single winner!'

'So, how do you explain the cash in your room?' demanded Bristow, annoyed by Robbie's intervention.

'What cash is that?'

'It was on your bedside table.'

'Oh! I always empty my pockets there, but I can't remember any money. To tell you the truth, I had a few yesterday, so it's all pretty blurry.'

'When was the last time you were in QuickMart, Lenny?'

'No idea! I sometimes pop in, as long as the manager isn't around.'

'Do you mean Matthew Walker?'

'That's him. A nasty piece of work. The world would be a better place without him.'

'Mr Peters,' said the duty solicitor in a warning tone, putting a restraining hand on Lenny's arm. 'He can take a running jump,' protested Lenny. 'He's a horrible man. I hate him!'

Bristow consulted his notes. 'We have witnesses that say you were in a tussle with him on Saturday night, and you made several threats in retaliation.'

'No. Don't remember that.'

'Also,' continued Bristow, 'We have two witnesses who say you were outside QuickMart on Sunday morning before the store would have opened, and you appeared to be unsteady on your feet, as though you were intoxicated. You shouted something unintelligible at them.'

'Ah, don't ask me! I don't remember a thing.'

'But we have been asking you, and you haven't given us a sensible answer. For that reason. Leonard Peters. I am charging you with the murder of Matthew Walker...'

Later, when Lenny had been returned to his cell, Bristow reflected on the case whilst Robbie finished writing the report.

Away with the fairies, that one. We'll have to watch that his solicitor doesn't play the medical or psychological card to reduce the sentence. In my book murder is murder, even if you can't remember doing it!

8

Tuesday

Ginny had scheduled this meeting with Julia the previous week, and the timing was perfect for Julia. She desperately needed to find a way to alleviate her stress.

'Oh Ginny,' she moaned, 'It's gone pear-shaped. What was the expression back in the day? It's all gone Pete Tong! Only a hundred times worse than that!'

'What's happened?' asked Ginny in alarm.

'Have you heard about Matthew Walker?'

'No, I've been up to my neck in receipts trying to sort my accounts out. I know of him, but I'm not sure if I've ever met him. He's the director of the theatre group you've been asked to help with, isn't he?'

'Was. He was the director. He's been murdered.'

'Oh, no! That's shocking! I can't believe it!'

'The police have arrested someone. A local drunk called Lenny. Do you know him?'.

'No, I don't. I daresay Adam will know him. He knows most people.'

'Anyway, Matthew ran the group in partnership with Patrick from the Library. I've spoken to him on the phone, and as you can imagine, he's very upset. And, to make matters worse, Patrick told me that all Stage Centre's assets have been frozen. So even though the actors are all volunteers, there's no money to continue with the play. Nothing to pay for the hire of the rehearsal room, costumes, props, publicity and the like. It's a complete disaster!'

'There must be a way around this,' responded Ginny.

'Another thing, Matthew was acting in *Deathtrap*, too. He was to play Porter, the attorney.'

'I'm so sorry, Julia. The best thing I can do right now is make a pot of tea. Here, have a cat. I find stroking Tuxie is an ideal way of relieving stress, and she likes it too!' Ginny transferred Tuxie from her own lap to Julia's and left the office to put the kettle on.

She soon returned with a tray, which she balanced on top of a pile of papers.

'I have some suggestions to make,' she said, 'First of all, I can invest a bit of money for some short-term expenses as long as I eventually get it back. And secondly - crowdfunding. Lots of arts projects depend on it - from funding films to making music.'

'But I wouldn't know where to start,' protested Julia.

'You might not, but your son, Rupert, would.'

'True,' said Julia, 'It would be a sight more useful than building online kingdoms or fighting virtual dragons.'

'And thirdly, what about Doc playing Porter, the attorney?'

'Do you think he would?'

'You can but ask!' replied Ginny.

'I've just had an idea,' said Julia, brightening up, 'There is a backstage guy, Chris, who wants to act. Maybe he could start as an understudy and Doc could coach him. Then, if it works out, they can swap later. I'm feeling better already. Thank you, Ginny. I can't remember what this meeting was supposed to be about.'

'Ha ha, nothing exciting, I'm afraid. As work is a little slow at the moment, I thought I would take this opportunity to update all of your CVs. I'll email you a draft to edit. I've already added your role as Assistant Director for *Deathtrap*, so we have to make it happen. Only I'll delete the word *assistant*.'

***

It didn't seem fair to Ginny that she couldn't claim back all the money she spent on tea as a tax allowance. Just as a truck couldn't run without diesel, she certainly couldn't work without being fortified with regular cups of tea. Her accountant had told her that she could claim back the cost of supplying her clients with tea and coffee when they visited, so now, armed with her appointments diary, she was wading through a quagmire of calculations trying to work out the actors' beverage consumption. It was a welcome interruption when her phone rang.

'Hello, Ginny.'

'Robbie. How nice to speak to you.'

'Just a quick call whilst my boss is out of the office. I presume you've heard about Matthew Walker's murder?'

'I have. Julia told me all about it. It's shocking. But you've caught the culprit, haven't you?'

'Yes. Well, maybe. That's why I'm ringing, actually. We've charged a local man called Lenny Peters with the murder, but there's something he said that is troubling me.'

'Go on.'

'This conversation mustn't get back to my boss, or I'll be up to my neck in the proverbial. It's just that Lenny said he spent Sunday at the races with an actor, so I thought who better to ask than you. The Sarge won't want me digging around. As far as he's concerned, he's cracked the case in double quick time, and he's expecting a pat on the back from the Chief.'

'I can certainly ask my clients, the Dead Actors, if any of them can corroborate Lenny's story,'offered Ginny.

'Even if he was at the races, it doesn't necessarily mean he's innocent. We haven't had the time of death confirmed by the pathologist yet. We are guessing that it was sometime on Sunday morning because we discovered that QuickMart never actually opened on Sunday, much to the annoyance of several regulars who now regret the names they called Mathew Walker at the time. Anyway, I would appreciate it if you could ask around. Lenny's brain is befuddled by drink, and maybe he did commit murder and then forgot about it, but it doesn't feel right to me not to explore every avenue.'

***

How to play: place your stake. Press launch. The rocket will weave its way through the asteroids and dock with the space station. If you connect, you win; if you miss, you will be lost in Space.

'This looks fun. I'll play just a couple of games. It's cheap entertainment. Level One to start, I'll bet a pound. You can't buy much for a pound these days, can you? And launch! Go, little rocket. Boldly go! Wow! That asteroid nearly knocked you off course. Yes! Made it, and I've doubled my stake. Another one! Here we go. Two pounds at risk, and we are flying at superspeed. Yes, Yes! The Force is with me. I've doubled my winnings. Let's try Level Two...

It has to be Level Three. Cowardice is the path to the dark side. I've lost a lot, but I can win it all back by being brave. Noooo! Where did that asteroid come from?'

***

'Hello.'

'Hi Ginny, nice of you to ring. How are you?'

'I'm fine, Adam. I wondered if you fancied coming with me to the Red Lion tonight. As it's a Tuesday, the Dead Actors will be there. Or have you got something else on?'

'No, no. I'd love to come - anything to drag me away from this computer. I've spent too long on it lately. It's not good for me! I'll put my winter jacket on. I can't believe this weather. I wonder what the odds are of getting to the end of June without a single warm, sunny day! I'll bet my right arm on it. Oh, no, wait a minute, I might need it in the pub. It wouldn't feel right lifting a beer with my left arm.'

***

Steve was the first to spot Ginny and Adam and he shuffled along the bench seat in the snug of the Red Lion.

'There's plenty of room for two more littl'uns! Budge up, guys,' he said to the other Dead Actors.

'Littl'un! I think you jest, kind Sir,' laughed Adam, patting his stomach and pulling up a stool while Ginny settled herself in next to Steve.

'I think Steve's trying to shift attention from his own growing mid section,' laughed Angie.

'Do you know, if you are trying for roles of more portly gentlemen, like Falstaff, for instance, instead of eating all those cakes at the garden centre cafe, you could just wear a fat suit,' suggested Doc.

'Oh no, my dear child,' cried Steve, adopting the fruity tone of a hammy Shakespearean actor, 'That simply wouldn't do. I'm a method actor, so eating all the cakes and pies is fundamental to my research!'

'Seriously though, Doc,' warned Julia, 'When you come along to the Stage Centre rehearsal, don't be making any jokes about being overweight. Apparently, Samantha got quite upset in the past about the cruel remarks that Matthew had made about her. Don't they call it fat shaming? Anyway, now that he's been murdered, she might feel guilty about the bitter feelings she had towards him. It's all best left alone.'

'Actually, I wanted to ask you all a question,' said Ginny. 'I don't want to go into details because it touches on information I shouldn't know about, and it may seem like a random question, but did any of you go horse-racing on Sunday?' Everyone shook their heads.

'Gym in the morning, Sunday lunch, then horizontal, inspecting the inside of my eyelids,' said Steve.

'Drove to Ikea to buy a lightbulb, Swedish meatballs for dinner, spent a hundred pounds on stuff I didn't need!' added Doc.

'Stood on a touchline watching my nephew play football in the morning, borderline hypothermia, burger from a pitchside van, recovering in the afternoon with the fire on, watching It's a Wonderful Life on TV,' said Julia.

'Flew to Saturn in the morning looking for an eternity ring, Kickapoo Joy Juice for lunch, stopped off at the moon in the afternoon to buy cheese. Oh, tell a lie, that was Saturday. I was weeding the allotment on Sunday,' contributed Angie.

Whilst Adam joined in with the laughter, a tiny part of him was disappointed. He might even have said slightly miffed, because he had assumed that Ginny had invited him to the pub because she wanted his company, whereas really she had wanted to ask the others about their whereabouts on Sunday. He quickly dismissed such negative feelings. *What right have I got to put constraints on our friendship? After all, I know what tremendous courage it takes for Ginny just to leave the security of her house.*

On the walk back, Ginny linked arms with Adam.

'I did enjoy this evening,' she said. 'I know I often say it, but we must do this more often. I have every intention, but somehow...' her voice tailed off. Adam patted her hand.

'You're doing just fine,' he reassured her.

'I hope you don't think I'm taking you for granted. I know that I couldn't do it without your support, but that's not the only reason I asked you along tonight. I love spending time with you.' Adam responded with another pat on her hand. When they reached Ginny's house, she turned to him.

'Adam, I would invite you in for a cup of coffee, but you know how much it takes out of me when I venture out. I'm exhausted. I need to go straight to bed.'

'That's alright. I've got something to do on the computer anyway. Do you still want me to come to see your accountant?'

'Please, if you don't mind.'

'Not at all. Till Thursday, then. Goodnight, Ginny.' Before she turned to walk through her garden gate, Ginny reached up and gave Adam a peck on the cheek.

'Goodnight,' she whispered.

***

'A quick ten pound spin before I go to bed.

Cherry, watermelon, lemon.

Orange, banana, cherry.

Grape, orange, banana.

Lemon, orange, lemon.

Cherry, cherry, watermelon

Aghhh! Nearly. I'll just have one more go.

…one more'.

9

Thursday

'I hope I've printed out everything I need. I'm terrified I'll lose everything if my computer breaks down.'

'I know exactly what you mean, Ginny,' said Adam, 'Computers! They can be your friend or your enemy. I've been spending a lot of time on mine lately, and it's not always been going so well. I'll tell you what - an old school pal of mine, Denny, has been in touch with me recently. He's a computer expert and is coming back to

Shepton Rise soon to do some work for the Town Council. I could ask him if he would take a look at your setup and make sure everything's backed up to the Cloud.'

'That would be fantastic,' replied Ginny.

'Although for me, rather than the Cloud, I'll see if he can link me up to a rainbow,' laughed Adam. 'I might find a pot of gold downloaded onto my laptop! Right, have we got everything? It's another cold, breezy day out there, and it looks like rain, so we had better take my car.'

Ginny smiled and saluted. 'Aye, aye, captain. Thank you for this, Adam. Twice in one week! I'm turning into a regular gadabout!'

'It was enjoyable the other night in the pub, wasn't it?' said Adam, as they climbed into his car, 'Mind you, you've got to keep your wits about you when the Dead Actors are on form. They are forever taking the mickey.'

'Stop!' shouted Ginny.

'But I haven't even put the key in the ignition yet! Do you want to call it off and go back inside? I don't mind.'

'No. It's what you just said,' replied Ginny excitedly.

'You've got to keep your wits about you?'

'No, you said "taking the mickey". I immediately wondered who Mickey was, and then, for some crazy reason, I thought Mickey rhymes with Ricky,' explained Ginny.

'True, but I don't get the significance of this tortuous train of thought!'

'It only just occurred to me that the actor Lenny claims to have gone to the races with might have been the enigmatic and highly unpredictable Ricky Flynn. I knew I felt unsettled and that I hadn't dotted all the i's and crossed all the t's. The idea must have been lurking at the back of my brain.'

'It's funny you should say that because Robbie was saying to me last night that he doesn't think Lenny is a murderer. He was hoping that when he sobered up, he would remember more, but Lenny's mind is still a bit of a black hole. Anyway, we had better be on our way to the accountant's, or we will be late.'

***

There were three floors of offices above Cooper's Estate Agents; accessed by a separate door. Ginny led Adam along a hallway leading to a back door and a flight of stairs. Graham Smith's office was on the first floor,' said Ginny.

'I've brought my friend Adam along. I hope that's okay?' said Ginny as they entered Graham Smith's office.

'Perfectly fine,' replied the accountant, 'We've met before, haven't we?' he said, holding out a hand to Adam. Adam balanced Ginny's documents on the edge of the desk and shook Graham's hand.

'Yes, that's right. When I worked as a travel agent, your father used to do my accounts. Only, he used to be upstairs, and wasn't the firm called Smith, Smith and Smith in those days?'

'Well remembered. There were three of us, with offices one above the other. My father died quite a few years ago, and my brother, Stephen, had a yearning to live by the sea. In his spare time, he spends his hours trying to, as he puts it, catch a wave.'

'He's a surfer!' cried Adam.

'Exactly. Whereas I spend my working days adding up numbers, and in my spare time I do crosswords. I've also recently discovered Sudoku,'

'More numbers,' commented Ginny.

'I suppose so. Anyway, although it can't compete with California, Stephen reckons the best surfing in this country is in Cornwall - which is hardly within commuting distance. So, I bought Stephen out, and he set up as an accountant down there. I renamed this company Abacus Accountants.'

'Very appropriate,' commented Adam.

'Yes, but not because of the number connection. It also means the name comes at the top of an alphabetical list.'

'I don't suppose many people use phone directories any more or even address books,' said Ginny sadly.

'You're right; all the contacts are in there,' said Adam, pointing at Graham's mobile phone, which was resting on the corner of his desk. 'And getting your name to the top of an internet search is all about keywords and SEOs and the like. Do you have a website?' He picked up a business card from the desk.

'All very basic, I'm afraid. I resisted having a mobile phone until quite recently, so I've had to get the cards reprinted and add the number. Keep it please, I've enough to last a lifetime! Anyway, splitting the business with Stephen was all very amicable. I'm just about to spend a long weekend with him actually. I would have gone during the bank holiday, but the weather was so awful that I postponed it. I'm shutting up shop tonight and driving down in the morning. Stephen still helps me out now and then when I get too busy.' Graham gestured behind him to the floor-to-ceiling shelves, stuffed with box files and manila folders.

'That seems to defy the laws of science!' laughed Ginny, 'I thought my office was crammed with documents, but this is on a different level!'

'Mr Smith, can I ask you something?' said Adam, 'I know this is Ginny's appointment, but I wondered if I might take a photograph of you. You see, I have this idea for a project taking photos of people in their workspace, and I think it would make a brilliant picture to have you sitting at your desk with all those files as a backdrop.'

'I've always considered myself as rather boring,' replied Graham, 'But I don't have any objections.'

'I'm trying to get the money together to buy a professional digital camera,' said Adam, 'For the moment, all I have is my phone, but this is too good an opportunity to miss.'

With the photograph taken, Graham took a look at Ginny's documents.

'Now, numbers - this is what I find interesting,' he purred.

***

'Graham's a funny old stick, isn't he?' said Ginny, stirring her cappuccino. She had felt an overwhelming sense of relief once she had handed her accounts over to Graham. As she was still feeling fairly relaxed about being out of the house, she and Adam had decided to seize the moment and call in at Nature Nurtures, the Garden Centre Cafe.

'Yes, Graham leads a rather narrow life. He and his brother seem to be like chalk and cheese. I can picture them on the beach in Cornwall, Graham in a pinstripe suit and Stephen in a tie-dyed pop festival tee shirt,' grinned Adam.

'Is Graham married, I wonder?' said Ginny.

'I shouldn't think so. Married to his calculator, perhaps. Hey Ginny, look at this photograph I took in his office. I think it's pretty good. I'll send him a copy. I wonder if he's got the hang of WhatsApp?' Adam studied Graham's business card, copied the phone number and sent him the photograph. A few minutes later, his phone pinged, and Adam glanced down to see that he had received a thumbs-up from Graham's number.

'Going back to what we were talking about earlier,' said Ginny, 'I'm going to give Ricky Flynn a ring, but not now, I'll wait until I get home. Thanks for the coffee, Adam. I can see why Steve comes here after every gym session - those cakes over there look delicious.'

'Then we will have to come back again,' smiled Adam.

10

Friday

Julia had spent a considerable amount of time choosing what to wear. She was very fond of the clothes she had put on first, a navy blue jacket and a pencil skirt, but when she looked in the mirror she realised they wouldn't do. *No, No, no. It's fine for a board meeting, but I look too intimidating. These are what I would wear if I wanted to reassure the men, then blindside them with a move they didn't see coming!* Outfit two only lasted a few seconds. *Oh no! It's a bit hippy chic. I want to be taken more seriously than this! Yes, I look like a creative free spirit, but I need to be listened to.* Eventually, Julia settled on an all-black outfit, allowing herself a splash of colour with a loosely-knotted scarf and an orange leather handbag.

The library was closed, but she knew Patrick was expecting her. There was much to discuss. She tried to visualise what he would look like and then stifled a gasp when the man who opened the door was exactly as she had imagined. He was balding, but not in a trendy, shaven style. His hair was receding on top, although still plentiful at the sides and back. Thick, horn-rimmed glasses served to give him a quiet intellectual air. Under a grey v-necked pullover, he wore a cream and blue checked shirt teamed with a navy polka-dot tie. It was as though he had stepped straight out of the 1950s.

'Hello, I'm Julia. It's very nice to meet you at last. Do you know, you remind me of...' Patrick held up a hand to stop her.

'I know. I remind you of Philip Larkin. Everybody says so. It's a lot to live up to,' he said sadly.

'Do you write poetry too?' asked Julia as she took a seat in Patrick's office.

'I'm afraid not,' he replied glumly, 'I studied literature at University, but although I was able to write essays about poets and writers, I soon learned that I didn't have that creative spark. I shared a dorm with

Matthew Walker at University and we made a good team. He was on a business course, but he was a talented actor. In those days, he was totally chaotic, while I was the organised and systematic one. We were quite a force in Kaleidoscope, our University drama group. When we left University, we had to earn a crust, so I got a job here. Then I had a bit of luck and came into some money, so Matthew came to Shepton Rise, got the job at QuickMart, took out a loan, and we set up Stage Centre. And the rest is history. Or it was. I'm so grateful to Mrs Fellows for stepping in to bankroll the next production, and to you for doing all the directorial work that Matthew would have done.'

'It must have been such a shock for you.'

'I can't describe how I feel. It's still hard to believe he's gone. I'm spending a lot of my time here, in the library, getting solace from my books,' replied Patrick, ruefully.

'So, we must talk about the production of *Deathtrap*. Ginny asked if you could give her a list of all the companies that are owed money so she can pay them directly. Ticket sales will go to her, and she will take out her expenses. She's not looking for any commission, she just wants to help - the show must go on!'

'Ginny is so generous. As our assets have been frozen, this is a lifeline,' said Patrick.

'I've been working with the whole cast, and I think it's going to be a great production. The actors have a lot of passion.'

The doorbell rang, and Patrick visibly flinched. 'Oh dear, I'm afraid we will have to curtail our meeting. I'm expecting a chap who is coming to upgrade our computer network.'

'That's okay,' said Julia, as they walked back through the library, 'I've got to be at a meeting at Ginny's soon anyway. It was so nice to meet you, Patrick. .'

'I love the colour of your bag, by the way, it goes so well with your scarf.'

'Why, thank you, Patrick.' *Result!* thought Julia

***

As Ginny brought in the tea and coffee, she recalled how worried she used to be at the thought of anyone invading her personal sanctuary. *It's different now; I'm so pleased to see the Dead Actors sitting around my dining room table.*

Even Tuxie seemed delighted with the arrival of the guests as she wound herself in and out of Ginny's legs, narrowly avoiding tripping her up.

'You like having all these laps to sit on, don't you, Tuxie? If you want to do that kneading thing you do with your paws, I suggest you start on Steve's lap.'

'Oy! I heard that!' yelled Steve.

'Here we all are again,' declared Doc, 'Reunited back in the incident room.' He turned to Ginny, 'So what's up, Doc? Oh no! That's your line, not mine. I'll get the hang of this acting business one day!'

Ginny laughed. 'Help yourselves to drinks. I'll tell you why I asked you all here. It concerns a person I perhaps met just a few times and another I never met at all. The first of these is the late Matthew Walker.' She taped a photocopy from the local newspaper over one of the framed portraits of her clients which lined the walls. 'I haven't got a photo of the second man, Lenny Peters, who has been arrested for Matthew's murder. The best I can do is this!' She stuck up an image she had printed from an internet search, of a man in a flat cap with a cigarette hanging from his bottom lip, a scarf knotted around his neck, a white shirt rolled up to the elbow, and black trousers with braces.

Steve laughed, 'That's an Andy Capp cartoon. I haven't seen one of those for years.'

'And no wonder!' scolded Angie, 'He wasn't

exactly a New Man. Work-shy, smoking, boozing and, particularly in the early cartoons, he thought it was quite acceptable to knock his wife around a bit.'

'Which is why I chose Andy Capp,' explained Ginny. 'Not that I know if Lenny has ever laid a finger on a woman, although Adam tells me he was a boxer in his youth. It is because Lenny is definitely not a New Man. Drinking and horse-racing seem to be his only pastimes. I also know he had a bit of a feud going on with Matthew, but he just seems too easy a fit for the murder.'

'And it's not just Ginny who is uneasy,' added Adam, 'I've known Lenny all my adult life, and he's never struck me as being someone capable of murder, and Robbie is also uncomfortable with the idea. However, he has to be careful not to step on his boss's toes. Detective Sergeant Bristow is convinced Lenny is guilty.'

Ginny nodded. 'One of the things we know, via Robbie, is that Lenny can't remember much about last Sunday. He swears he was at the races with an actor, which was why I asked you all where you were on Sunday.'

'And here's me thinking you were trying to put me in the frame for the murder,' quipped Steve.

'Your ugly mug is already in a frame, up there,' laughed Julia, pointing to Steve's publicity shot for the *City Beat Blue* TV series.

'This would be a nice twist; good cop turns bad, but what would my motive be?'

'I know!' cried Doc, 'You accuse him of trying to harm you by selling you a packet of out-of-date chocolate chip cookies, and then...'

'Please, guys, can we stick to the script?' interrupted Ginny. 'So then I realised yesterday that there is another actor I had forgotten about - Ricky Flynn!'

'Oh Lord, a real loose cannon,' laughed Steve.

'I saw him in that film, *Peter Pan and the Lost Toys*,' said Angie.

'He was miscast,' commented Julia, 'He shouldn't have been Captain Hook. It's Ricky who doesn't want to grow up and still acts like a teenager - distracted by pretty girls, loud music and excited because he's found the key to the drinks cabinet!'

'He's practically a lost boy himself,' added Doc.

'And so,' said Ginny in a loud voice to quieten the room, 'And so I rang him up last night and I was eventually able to get to the bottom of it. Ricky didn't even know Lenny's name.'

'I'd be surprised if he knew his own name!' laughed Angie. 'Sorry, Ginny. Carry on,'

'Ricky picked Lenny up in a taxi from outside QuickMart on Sunday morning, and they spent the whole day together at Brinloss Race Course, returning in the evening.'

'So that's it then,' said Steve, 'Lenny's got an alibi.'

'It's not as straightforward as all that,' explained Adam, 'I've spoken to Robbie about it. 'First of all, the police are still waiting for the coroner's report - the time of death has not been established yet. So, it is possible Lenny could have murdered Matthew before Ricky took him to the races. Also, there is no actual evidence they were together and, finally, Ricky is not exactly the most reliable of witnesses.'

'I think we have to hang fire and carry out our own investigations,' said Ginny, 'At least Lenny will be getting fed where he is and have the chance to dry out. Also, the real murderer might get complacent knowing someone else has been arrested for the crime.'

'Where do we start?' asked Doc.

'I think one thing you can say about murders in small towns is that, generally, the murderer knows the victim, and the community knows the murderer too,' Steve said confidently. 'It's not like some random attack by a maniac that might happen in a city. I'm speaking from years of experience as a TV cop, of course, so you can take my word for it!'

'I remember in my cafe in *The Street*, a couple came in for breakfast,' offered Angie. 'He said to her, *I love you, parsnip*, and she replied, *I love you, Funny Bunny*. Then she jumped up, brandished a gun, and shouted, *Okay, everybody, chill, this is a robbery!* Oh no, maybe not. I think I'm remembering a movie, and I wasn't even in it!'

'Well,' said Doc, ' In my series I had to deal with the other end of the scenario,' I remember one time when I had to spend hours in theatre trying to patch together this woman who had been thrown off a tall building. All I succeeded in doing was missing my dinner. The canteen had closed by the time we finished filming.'

'Are you sure that wasn't me?' asked Julia, 'I got written out of *Stirling Heights* when I got thrown off a skyscraper,'

'I don't know,' replied Doc, 'It was before we met. It might have been. Do you have a tattoo of a heart just above...'

'I wouldn't tell you if I had!' snapped Julia, 'Anyway, how is this helping us find out who killed Matthew?'

'If nothing else, it's getting your brains into gear,' observed Ginny. 'Julia, I was wondering if your Rupert might lend a hand in case we need to strengthen Lenny's alibi. I hesitate to call Ricky Flynn a talented actor, but he is certainly a recognisable one among the young followers of his genre, often girls likely to be on social media. So maybe Rupert could trawl through the internet and see if he can find any photos from the trip to the races, perhaps a selfie?'

'What self-respecting, trendy young girl wouldn't want a selfie of herself with Lenny,' laughed Angie.

'Adam,' Ginny continued, 'It's just occurred to me that maybe Lenny would give us a key and permission to have a look in his room. Perhaps you could ask Robbie. The police were looking for evidence to incriminate Lenny, like the cash they found, but we would be looking for evidence to prove his innocence.' Adam nodded his agreement. 'I don't think Matthew's assistant, Elsie Godwin, is involved,' Ginny went on, 'Robbie told me the police investigated her, and her alibi looks solid as she was on holiday at the time of the murder. The only other person who works at QuickMart is the storeman, Gerry Wilkinson, but he was admitted to hospital on Saturday night, so it's definitely not him.'

'Don't tell me, he was suffering from heatstroke after all this glorious weather we have been having,' suggested Steve, looking out at the rain pelting the window.

'No, it was a more delicate condition than that. Let me just say he has eight children, and his wife does not want any more!'

'Ow!' Doc winced, 'Luckily, I never had to perform one of those!'

'So,' said Ginny, 'What I'm saying is, I'm narrowing the pool of suspects down to the am-dram actors from Stage Centre. They probably all knew the best and the worst of Matthew.'

'Doc and I will be working with them at the rehearsal tomorrow afternoon,' said Julia.

'As your plan is to work towards getting Chris on stage, I wonder if you could ask if they would like me to come along so he could train me to operate the lights?' Steve suggested.

'Any opportunity to be near a spotlight!' observed Angie wryly.

'Come along anyway, I'm sure they won't say no,' suggested Julia.

'Everybody. Keep your ears and eyes open,' said Ginny, 'If the murderer is one of them, you mustn't arouse any suspicions.'

***

As the Dead Actors were walking home, Angie spoke up.

'I've just been thinking,' she said.

'Ooh, I wouldn't do that, dear.' Julia laughed, 'We only get a finite number of thoughts before our brain becomes jelly. I wouldn't waste any of them on us!' .

'Does the blancmange stage come before or after that?' asked Steve.

'Blancmange! What is the point? It sits there, pale and quivering. Looking at you with evil intent!' said Doc.

'There's a bull terrier down our road that sounds just like that!' said Julia.

'I mean, blancmange! For goodness sake, it's tasteless!'

'It suits those novelty socks you're wearing, Doc,' quipped Steve.

'How very droll,' replied Doc, airily.

'Anyway, I've been thinking about the storeman at QuickMart,' continued Angie, 'I've never met him...'

'Don't you think an online dating site might be a surer bet?' interrupted Steve.

'I didn't think he was your type!' commented Julia,

'I thought you liked them tall, dark and handsome, but he's got a shock of red hair and freckles!'

'As I was saying,' Angie went on, 'Even though he was in hospital at the time of the murder, it might be useful if I had a chat with him. Maybe he could tell us about anyone else with a grudge against Mathew.'

'Yes, good idea,' said Julia, patting Angie on the head, 'It's not all blancmange in there after all!'

***

"As we approach the end of the week, the weather improves with more sunshine and warmer temperatures. While northern and western areas may experience some rain, high pressure from the southwest will bring drier conditions. Saturday will be sunny in the south, with rain mainly in the north and west."

11

Saturday

'At last, sunshine! That's got to bring me luck. I'll try a few slots - nice, bright, and shiny to suit the weather. But first, I'm going to watch a video blog.'

"...that is the wild function that makes this game amazin'. So when you see those diamonds right there in the middle, that's literally like a wild line. So Diamond Dust plays out on five reels, right, with ten pay lines, and you win both ways, but the real juice. I mean, the real, real action is when you get a wild re-spin. That's when you get a row of diamonds, with an entire line being wild for you, and then there's a re-spin to see if anything matches up for you. If you hit a win on that one, you'll get another Diamond Dust re-spin stacking up on your previous win. Oh! There we go! Activation baby! Oh, man, a combo. Can there be more? Can there be more? Oh Dude. As if on cue, baby. Megawin! And this is why I love this game. Four hundred and twenty bucks. Just like that!"

***

The little group of friends took varying amounts of time and attention to get ready every day. Unless Ginny was leaving the house, she was happy to slop around in an oversized sweatshirt over a stretchy tee shirt and leggings. Now that she had incorporated yoga into her daily routine, it was especially suitable; she could remove a layer to start her exercises and put her top back on for her savasana relaxation pose at the end. On the rare occasion when Adam joined her, that was the moment when, lying outstretched on his back, he invariably fell asleep.

Julia would readily admit that she took far longer to get ready than she ought to. Quite frequently, the outfit that she ended up wearing was the first thing that she had tried on, but she couldn't reach that decision without first studying herself in the mirror in a range of clothes. She wasn't being vain - she was trying to analyse what conveyed the particular mood of the forthcoming event, even if she was just visiting Heavenly Delights to buy cakes. One thing you could predict about Julia is that she always looked smart.

The same couldn't be said about Angie. Some might say her clothes were mismatched. She preferred to think her style was individual and inspirational. Her go-to choice was one of the many pairs of dungarees in her overstuffed wardrobe. She had favourites: the ones printed with sausage dogs frequently got an airing. She swore that Tuxie avoided her when she wore those, yet the cat would happily curl up on her lap when she wore the ones with images of constellations, flowers, or even leopardskin! *You would think Tuxie would be afraid of bigger cats, but maybe she has never met one!*

Of the men, the most predictable was Steve. No one could remember the last time anyone saw him sporting anything other than the police-style black shoes he wore on set for City Beat Blue, a blue shirt, black trousers and a black tie. If it was a really hot summer's day, he might ditch the tie and wear a short-sleeved shirt, but never shorts. Not unless he was on holiday in Brittany, where he thought no one would recognise him.

While Steve had a lot of clothes that looked the same, Doc had a range of clothes that were suitable for various occasions. It was nowhere near as extensive as Julia's wardrobe, for he switched between five suits, with Suit Number One being the most elegant and Suit Number Five quite shabby and only worn if he wanted to audition for the role of a down-and-out. In more casual situations, he chose between jackets numbered one to five. The best of these was a Harris Tweed jacket, particularly useful if he wanted to play a member of the gentry, perhaps on a shoot or at a country fair. Number Five was once an expensive jacket from Holland & Holland, now frayed and with leather patches at the elbows. Doc lived in the hope of being called to audition for Lady Chatterley's Lover - he could certainly pass for a gamekeeper, if not, perhaps, for a lover!

As for Adam, it was rare that he wasn't wearing a band tee shirt, even if it was hidden underneath several layers of clothing. Sometimes, he bought them from online vintage shops. More prized were those that were souvenirs from gigs that he had attended when he was younger. Some of them, like the one he wore today, were purchased as merchandise during reunion tours when those same bands returned to the UK to perform their greatest hits.

Adam unzipped his jacket, partly because it was quite warm in the cafe and partly because he wanted to expose his Foo Fighters tee shirt. He might be on the wrong side of fifty, but the shirt proclaimed that he was still young at heart.

'Hey, Denny. It's good to see you again. It's been a long time. Brunch was a great idea,' said Adam. The two old friends embraced.

'Yeah. Good to see you, too. It's not too early for you, is it? I haven't disturbed your Saturday lie-in?' asked Denny.

'Heavens no! I've been up for ages. I was doing some stuff on the computer, but it didn't go too well, so I wish I'd stayed in bed!' Denny looked around the cafe.

'I haven't been back to Shepton Rise for years, not since my parents moved South. I don't remember all this.'

'It was just operating as a garden centre in those days. That was before it rebranded. They built this place and expanded the gift shop. Now it's a destination for people like us who have no intention of walking out with a plant.'

Ten minutes later, after they had ordered food, their conversation resumed.

'How are you finding it being back in the sticks after working in London all this time?' asked Adam.

'It's all good. When this project came up, I jumped at the chance to come back and relive old memories.'

'So what exactly are you doing for the Town Council? Computer stuff, I presume.' asked Adam.

'Yes, that's right. I suppose you might loosely define it as *safeguarding*. I'm looking at the computers in the council offices and the library and checking to ensure they aren't being misused or hacked, and I'm installing systems to protect the public and employers.'

'Rock and Roll!' laughed Adam.

Denny smiled. 'Hey do you remember that school band we were in?. Three chords and no idea! What were we called? I know! *Losing Streak.*'

'Yeah. That figures! We were pretty useless.'

***

Flowers or chocolates? Angie deliberated, then plumped for chocolates and called in at the newsagents. Then, she had another decision to make, *Dark or milk? Well, I like milk chocolates, you never know, he might offer me one. Now then, soft centre or nutty. No contest - who has a strawberry cup out of choice? No one I know!* Taking her selection to the counter, Angie noticed a newspaper headline quoting a politician: "Difficult Choices, Tough Decisions". *You're not kidding! World peace? Climate change? Tax cuts? Easy-peasy compared with choosing between a Hazelnut Cluster and a Caramel Surprise!*

On her way to the hospital, Angie met a nurse who was about to start her shift.

'Excuse me, can you tell me which ward someone would be in after a vasectomy?' she asked.

'Most likely be taken to the Camembert Ward on the first floor.'

'Camembert?'

'Don't ask! It's because we are twinned with a French city, so someone had the bright idea of naming the wards after French cheeses!' replied the nurse, rolling her eyes.

'Is it reciprocated?' laughed Angie, 'Salle de Sausage Roll, perhaps, or Service de Poisson et Frites!'

Angie skipped up the stairs and followed the signs to the Camembert Ward.

Julia told me I can't miss him - unruly red hair and freckles. Unfortunately, there was no one of that description in the Camembert ward, although there was one patient who had been bandaged from head to foot. *He seems to be asleep, so I suppose I could peel a few bandages back and have a peek at the colour of his hair, but surely that would be some overzealous bandaging after a vasectomy.* The next bed was empty and the rest of the room was occupied by men with every possible hair colour except red. Angie tried the Brie ward without success, then Edam. *Edam! Someone doesn't know their Geography!* Finally, Angie ended up back at Camembert. She was just contemplating unwrapping Mr Bandage when she saw the nurse she had talked to earlier.

'I can't find him. Can you help? His name is Gerry Wilkinson.' The nurse smiled and retrieved a list of patients from the office.

'I can't see him,' she said, 'What time was his operation?'

'I don't know what time. It was last Saturday,' replied Angie.

'Saturday! They are sent home within twenty-four hours after a vasectomy.'

'What! After all that delving around...down there!'

'That's right, love. If they have to go home on the bus, they usually bring a cushion to sit on.'

'Ah, well! Would you like a chocolate?'

'I don't mind if I do,' replied the nurse, looking over her shoulder to check that her superiors weren't nearby. 'I don't suppose there is a strawberry cup, is there? They're my favourites!'

*****

It was time for a break. The other members of Stage Centre had returned to the rehearsal room, but Julia, Doc and Steve lingered by the vending machines in the Corny reception to chat in private.

'How's it going?' asked Julia.

'It's quite difficult operating with two hats on. As far as the play is concerned, then fine. The lines are pretty much in there already,' said Doc, tapping his forehead, and I've read through the play numerous times. It's trying to draw conclusions about whether any of the actors are murderers that's difficult.'

'Two hats? I recommend that to look like a detective, one of your hats should be a fedora,' said Steve. 'Then maybe I should follow Sherlock's example and wear a deerstalker.'

'Very helpful!' retorted Julia, 'Now focus, for goodness sake. You've both met Ashley from Heavenly Delights before. Do you think she seems a bit on edge?'

'Yes, I do,' replied Doc. 'Obviously though, she might just be upset about Matthew's death and/or, be nervous about being in the play,'

'Actually, I've never met Chris before, but he seems a bit jumpy,' observed Steve, 'It could be that he is feeling guilty for killing Matthew, or maybe he too has stage fright. He's held a grudge about being prevented from acting for so long that now taking to the stage is a reality, perhaps he's not sure he's up to it.'

'I'm not sure what actor's hat Doc ought to wear,' mused Steve as they walked back to the rehearsal room, 'It depends on your vision for the play, oh great and mighty director.'

'Unless you two behave, I'll make it a sequel to *Planet of the Apes*, and you'll have to wear monkey suits,' said Julia sternly. 'Shush now.'

The three walked quietly into the rehearsal room so as to observe the body language of the rest of the cast. Jack and Samantha were each silently studying the script, but Ashley and Chris were having a whispered conversation at the far end of the room. Julia clapped her hands.

'OK, guys, we'll continue with the read-through. As before, Steve will take the part of Clifford, as Jay isn't back from Uni yet, but this time, Chris, how about you tackle Porter's role?' Chris nodded nervously. 'Let's backtrack a little and start from where Porter enters for the first time. Cue the doorbell.'

'I haven't made one yet,' said Chris.

'I'll do it,' announced Steve, 'Ding, dong, ding dong,' he sang out, then just as Samantha opened her mouth to speak, he continued, 'Ding, dong, ding dong.' Julia wagged a finger at him, and murmured:

'Monkey suit.' Doc burst out laughing, while the others looked confused. 'Carry on.' said Julia, 'Assume that the doorbell has just rung.'

'Hello, Porter,' said Chris.

'That's my line,' snapped Samantha.

'Oh! Sorry. Hello Myra.'

'No, wait until I've said my line, and it's not "Hello Myra" anyway, it's Good evening, Myra.'

'Guys, guys!' said Julia soothingly. Let's start again.Take it slowly, and remember we are not trying to do it from memory. It's a read-through. From the top.'

'Ding, dong, ding dong,' carolled Steve. Julia closed her eyes.

An hour later the rehearsal was over and a caretaker arrived to lock up. Steve was the first to leave the room, not because he was in any hurry to go home, but because he regretted having drunk a large coffee earlier and was rushing off to find a bathroom. When he emerged into the corridor, he heard voices ahead coming from around a corner. Chris and Ashley had evidently imagined everyone else had left the building. Feeling a little guilty, Steve tiptoed closer to eavesdrop.

'Are you sure you've not told a soul?' breathed Ashley, 'Not anyone in your family?'

'No, definitely not. It's been difficult at times and I nearly let it slip once, but no,' replied Chris.

'Good! It has to remain a secret, or else everything will be ruined,' insisted Ashley.

'What do you want me to do about the cash? I presume we are dividing it equally?'

'Yes, half and half. Let's sort it out here tomorrow. If we come at one o'clock, there will be no one else here. Did you manage to wash your clothes, Chris? I've never seen such a mess! You didn't just put them in the laundry bin, did you?'

'I put them in a bin bag and threw them out. Took a long time to scrub my hands. Then I had to wash the basin because it was stained red.'

'Well, that would arouse suspicion in itself,' laughed Ashley, 'I bet you've never done that before either!'

'True.' Chris muttered, 'Come on, let's go before we get locked in.'

Steve's heart pounded in his chest as the voices faded, the weight of the overheard words pressing heavily upon him. He remained still, taking shallow breaths as he waited for the footsteps to recede into the distance.

12

Sunday

Five determined people formed a chevron as they advanced quietly along the corridor to break up Chris and Ashley's secret meeting.

At the head of the "V" strode Robbie; for once, he wasn't wearing his heavy police-issue boots because he was off-duty, so walking silently was not as problematic as usual. He had been conflicted about how to respond to the information that Ginny had given him but decided that, rather than risk annoying Bristow by going through police channels and appearing to be insubordinate, it would be better to take this low-key approach.

To his right marched Steve. Ironically, he was the one wearing police boots, for he had dozens of pairs from his time as Jack Dempster in *City Beat Blue*, but walking without making a noise came easily to him. Years of complaints from the sound technicians on film sets about his *clodhoppers* had ensured that, just like the *Pirates of Penzance*, he walked with cat-like tread. Steve was wondering to himself whether this might be the first time a weak bladder had played a part in catching murderers. He would never have heard the whispered conversation between Ashley and Chris if he hadn't needed to find the washroom.

Adam was on Robbie's left. He had mixed emotions. Although he was proud that his son was taking the lead in this exercise, and appreciated the chance to support Ginny, he was worried about their mission; he accepted that murderers shouldn't be allowed to get away with it, but he genuinely liked Chris and Ashley. On a selfish level, if Ashley was in prison, where would Adam buy chocolate Florentine biscuits from in the future?

Julia walked behind Steve. The Dead Actors had debated whether they should all join this posse. They decided that having a second woman with them might have a calming influence on events and agreeed that Julia would be best suited because she had formed a bond with Chris and Ashley. Julia kept saying to herself, What a waste, what a waste. It was like a mantra to steady her nerves, but it was also what she felt about the actors' potential, because she genuinely sensed a spark of untapped talent in Ashley and Chris.

Lastly, slightly behind Adam, walked Ginny. She would have liked to reach out and hold Adam's hand for reassurance, but thought it wouldn't be appropriate. She had only met Ashley on a few occasions and didn't know Chris at all, so she had no firm preconceptions about them other than what Julia had told her. She knew that Chris had resented Matthew for preventing him from acting and that Ashley had been wounded by Matthew's remarks about her weight, so revenge was a possible motive for both of them. In addition, the conversation that Steve had overheard appeared to reveal their guilt. One advantage of having the conversation relayed to her by Steve was Ginny knew that an actor's account could be relied upon to be word-perfect, with every inflection mimicked and variations in tone captured accurately.

Ginny hadn't expected it all to happen so quickly.

She tried not to reveal to the Dead Actors, and even to Adam sometimes, just how difficult it was for her to leave the house. She had developed various strategies to calm her fears of having a panic attack - from changes to her diet and regular yoga sessions to using visualisation techniques, but she usually had more time to prepare herself for stressful situations. Not now. The moment of truth had arrived.

The group rounded the corner and then let out a collective gasp. Standing on a chair to one side of the door of the function room was Chris. On the other side of the entrance, balanced on a small step ladder, was Ashley, and between them was suspended a large banner proclaiming, in drippy red paint, "Happy Birthday, Mark and Amy". Ashley turned at the sound of footsteps, wobbled, and then slipped awkwardly down the steps.

'Oops! That was a close one! Hello, you've come an hour too early for the surprise party, but you can lend a hand now you are here,' she chirped. 'It was a bit ambitious of us to think that we could get set up all by ourselves.'

The cold realisation washed over the group that there was another interpretation of the conversation Steve had overheard. Adam was the first to react.

'Sorry, we got the time wrong, but we're happy to help.

'My hubby's birthday is actually tomorrow, but Chris's wife, Amy, has hers today, and as they are only a day apart, it's a perfect opportunity to have a joint party. Nice to see you, Robbie.'

'I've been enjoying your honey flapjacks,' said Robbie cheerfully. Here, let me pin that up. I'm taller than you.'

'You're taller than everyone,' laughed Ashley. She looked around the rest of the group. The rest of the theatre gang was coming, but she couldn't remember if she had said anything to Steve and Julia. She presumed Chris had invited them. Chris was thinking along the same lines, imagining that Ashley had invited them. Actually, neither of them really cared if there were extras. It was a party - the more, the merrier.

'Welcome, everyone,' said Chris cheerfully. He caught Ginny's eye, 'Hello, I don't think we've met.'

'I'm Ginny.'

'Ginny is Stage Centre's financial backer, or "angel" as we say in the business,' explained Julia.

'Oh, how appropriate! I'm so pleased to meet you. We are all so grateful,' responded Ashley. Adam looked over towards Ginny. Beads of sweat lined her top lip and all the colour had drained from her face.

'Are you okay, Ginny?'

'Actually, I feel a little dizzy. I need to sit down.' Adam and Steve guided Ginny to a chair, and she sat with her head between her knees while she tried to control her breathing.

'Is there anything we can do,' asked Ashley.

'Ginny gets these episodes sometimes,' explained Adam.

'I'm sorry, I just need to get home and lie down,' whispered Ginny, straightening up. 'I don't feel so dizzy anymore.'

'Steve and I will help you back,' said Adam.

'My car is parked right outside,' added Steve. 'We'll take it slowly.'

'I'm sorry to be a party pooper,' said Ginny weakly, 'You two can come back after. The only company I'll need is Tuxie. I'll be fine. Sorry for all the drama.'

***

"After a pleasant but cold day yesterday, today brings low pressure and a windy afternoon. Cloud will increase, with rain mainly in the North and West, possibly heavy at times. Temperatures will drop due to the lack of sunshine."

***

'Hello… Police. I'd like to report a missing

person.'

13

Monday, Week Three.

Angie rubbed her hands together to warm them up. *We had some nice weather yesterday, and now it's freezing again! I wish I had put on a winter coat!* For once, Angie wasn't wearing her trademark dungarees but had chosen a simple grey skirt, a white shirt and a black cotton jacket. She carried a smart, black briefcase.

Elsie, deputising as temporary manager of QuickMart, had told her which road Gerry Wilkinson lived on.

'I don't know the number, dear, but you can't miss

it. It's got a red front door and probably toys all over the front lawn!'

As Angie walked along the road, she noticed a man walking in the opposite direction on the other side. He was wearing what seemed to be the uniform of men in the building trade these days: baggy tracksuit bottoms and a paint-splattered hoody, with a heavy lumberjack shirt over the top. His was red and black. He was carrying a plastic sandwich box and a flask. The toot of a horn drew Angie's attention to the approach of a battered van, with *Hammertime Construction: You Can't Touch Us*, painted on the side. The man climbed in, and the van roared away, loud rap music pumping out of the open window. Angie turned her attention back to looking for Gerry's house and found she had almost walked straight past it. Elsie had been right about the state of the front garden.

To say that the woman who answered the door looked tired would be an understatement. *After all, eight kids, no wonder!*

'Yes. Can I help you?' From inside, Angie could hear the sounds of World War Three erupting. One child was screaming, and another was shouting, 'Mam, Mam, Mam, Mam!'

'Sorry to trouble you, Madam,' said Angie sweetly,

'I wonder if I could have a word with Gerry Wilkinson. Just a follow-up after his operation. I've got some I.D. somewhere.' Julia started to rummage in her briefcase.

'Don't bother, love. He's out. For a start, everyone calls him Wilko, and he might still be waiting for his lift on the street. You can't miss him. He's wearing a red and black shirt. Now, if you don't mind, I had better sort this lot out!' As Angie retreated, she could hear Mrs Wilko shouting, 'How many times have I told you? I'll give you something to cry about in a minute!' The street was empty.

Damn. That builder I saw a minute ago was walking in a funny way. I thought he was swaggering, but in retrospect, he was waddling!

'I'm not exactly sure what to do,' said Angie to Steve later, 'It's Wilko, that's Gerry's nickname. I suspect he is moonlighting. Perhaps he's claiming sick pay from QuickMart and working on a building site.'

'You're not in a position to do anything because you don't know for certain what he's up to. You still want to talk to him about Matthew's murder, so why don't you do that and then decide?' suggested Steve.

'I might be able to kill two birds with one stone. I'll be better prepared tomorrow.'

✳✳✳

Once a fortnight, Mandy Heaton came to clean Ginny's house. Mandy had a team of cleaners working for her, but always made sure she was the only one who came to Ginny's. Mandy appreciated not only that Ginny found it difficult to leave her house, but also that only recently had she felt able to cope with outsiders venturing inside. Generally, when Mandy was cleaning, Ginny retreated to her office, which was off-limits to Mandy. Having peeked round the door, and given that her company was called *Clean and Tidy*, that was a source of regret for Mandy. Ginny's office was only borderline clean and a long, long way from being tidy!

Mandy loved her job; she could scrub and dust, polish and wax all day long, and frequently did unless someone brought her a cup of tea. Then, her other talent had a chance to shine, for Mandy loved to chat.

'I've brought you a mug of tea,' said Ginny, setting a tray down, 'And I've poured one for myself.' Ginny plopped herself down on one of the conservatory chairs. Mandy rarely sat down with a client; if she remained standing, it felt like she was still working.

'How are you liking the weather?' Ginny asked.

'Well, it was alright first thing this morning, it was quite cool then, but now the sun has come out, oh no.

It's too hot for me. I'm dripping!'

'Oh dear, I think it's too hot for those flowers as well.' Ginny pointed to the vase of wilting sweet williams, 'I think they need throwing out.'

'You'll have to drop a few hints to Adam.' Ginny knew there was no point in trying to keep her growing relationship with Adam a secret from Mandy. Mandy and her team were in and out of many households in the town, so Mandy was a fount of local knowledge. Some might call it gossip.

'I will,' laughed Ginny. 'Actually, it was Adam who bought me those - from Bloomin' Marvellous. Do you know Samantha Drake, who runs the shop?'

'I know her very well. I had quite a long chat with her the other week!' Ginny smiled encouragingly. This was precisely why she had engineered the teatime chat.

'Was she on good form?'

'Well, no. She was a bit down, to tell you the truth. It's quite a tragic story. Did you know that she and Matthew Walker, God rest his soul, were an item once?'

'Were they?' exclaimed Ginny. Actually, Ginny had heard about their relationship from Julia but thought it best to feign surprise. 'No doubt she was upset about Matthew's murder?'

'Hmmm, that wasn't why she was feeling sad. When she and Matthew were together, Samantha's sister came to stay, and she later admitted to Samantha that Matthew had, how can I put it, dallied in her direction. Obviously, Samantha was not best pleased. She broke off with Matthew and had a big row with her sister. But this is the tragic part - her sister left and then, a week later, was killed in a road accident. They never got the chance to make up before her sister was so cruelly snatched away. Deep down, Samantha blamed Matthew for that, and now he's gone too.'

'What a sad tale,' said Ginny.

'I know. She told me all this in the cemetery. I was there cleaning my parents' gravestone and she was doing the same for her sister, who is buried there. It was the anniversary of her sister's death last Sunday - the same day Matthew died. Anyway, I'd better get on. Can I put the radio on? I think I need something upbeat to get me going!'

In the kitchen, washing the mugs, Ginny recognised the song playing on the radio. It was *Cell Block Tango* from the musical *Chicago*, and the refrain in the chorus, *He had it comin'*, invaded Ginny's thoughts. On the one hand, she felt desperately sorry for Samantha, but on the other, it wasn't Matthew who had killed her sister. If Samantha had taken it upon herself to get her revenge by killing him, then that wasn't right. It wasn't justice!

***

Mandy had left and Ginny was pacing, too unsettled to get on with her work. *What should I do? The simplest thing would be to pass the information on to the police, but they already have Lenny in custody for the offence and are not looking for anyone else. This matter needs handling with sensitivity. I know there are police officers trained to deal with such a situation, but what if it was Detective Sergeant Bristow who ended up trampling all over Samantha's feelings in his size nine police boots? What to do?'*

Ginny sent Julia a text.

'Am I right in thinking you have a rehearsal today?'

'Yes, just with Samantha and Jack at two o'clock.'

'I want to have a private chat with Samantha. Would that work?'

'We can make it work. See you at two.'

***

Julia introduced Ginny to Samantha and Jack, and then Julia took her male lead to a corner of the room to do some work on accents. Julia had to decide whether to set *Deathtrap* in the Hamptons or ship it across the Atlantic to a wealthy English suburb. In the previous rehearsal Jack had sounded more like a Brooklyn gangster than a New York playwright. Meanwhile, Samantha and Ginny sat at the other end of the room. As an amateur actor, Samantha was thrilled to be in the presence of a bona fide theatrical agent.

Ginny was struggling to appear calm. She had decided it wouldn't be appropriate for Adam to be here, as there was no good reason for him to be in the rehearsal room. Also, Ginny didn't want to be a burden to Adam yet again, so she had steeled herself to come alone. She didn't have a plan of action - she was in unfamiliar territory. She needed to strike the balance between a chat and an interrogation, so she almost cried with relief when Samantha's opening remark allowed her to steer the conversation in the right direction.

'Are you alright now? I heard you came to Ashley and Chris's surprise party but left because you felt ill. You had already gone by the time I got there.' It was the moment for Ginny to be honest, open up, and see where the journey took her.

'I'm not sure that feeling ill is the best way of describing it. You see, externally, I may seem a confident creature, but underneath it all, I have irrational fears that I have to...I won't say conquer, that's setting the bar too high. I think control would be a better word to use.'

'Oh, how awful for you,'

'It is a strain. I wasn't always like this, but then there was a tragedy in my life.' Ginny paused a moment before adding, 'You see, my husband died in an accident, and ever since then...' she let her voice trail off. Samantha's eyes turned glassy and her bottom lip trembled. Despite feeling guilty about upsetting Samantha, Ginny pressed on because she needed to get to the truth. 'I'm very sorry,' she said, 'Have I touched a nerve.'

'It's, it's just that tragedy has touched my life too,' Samantha stammered, 'My sister had a car accident and we weren't on good terms when she passed. I never had the chance to make up.'

'Oh, I am sorry to hear that. But you can't blame yourself.'

'But I do. If I had never got together with Matthew Walker, we wouldn't have fallen out.'

'Did your sister not like him?'

'It was just the opposite. They had a fling.'

'But surely that wasn't your fault either.'

'If I think rationally, I agree, but it's still difficult.'

'How did it make you feel about Mathew?'

'I was angry at first and then deeply disappointed in Matthew. I had already broken it off before she died.'

'It was brave of you to stay with Stage Centre.'

'If I'd left, it would have seemed as though he had won. I would certainly have been the loser because I like being on stage so much.'

'Good for you!'

'I'm certain that he felt guilty, although he wasn't the kind of man who was prepared to admit it,' continued Samantha, 'Why else did he always give me the leading roles when sometimes Ashley would have been better suited for them? Even though Ashley's not said as much to me, I know that's an issue with her.'

'And how do you feel about Matthew now that he is dead?' Ginny asked gently.

'It's all a bit of a tangle. I'm ashamed to say that sometimes I feel like it's divine retribution, but mostly, I think it's all been such a waste,' Samantha replied sadly, dabbing her eyes with a tissue.

After Samantha joined Julia to continue rehearsing, Ginny reflected on the conversation. *Deep down, I don't think Samantha is the murderer, but I must keep in mind that Samantha is well-practised at manipulating the emotions of her audience.*

14

Monday

'You can sort this out at the end of your shift,' Bristow had said, 'I'm blowed if I'm going all the way to Shepton Rise to look for some old geezer who's probably just forgotten to plug in his phone!' Robbie was quite pleased about this end to his day. He always found it calming to be back in his home town after a stint in the city, and now he was back even earlier than usual.

He had already visited the home address. It was a

bungalow in Laurel Close, a 1960s property on a large plot, of a type much loved by the older folk in the town and even more coveted by developers who, given the chance, would knock it down and put up two houses in the same spot. He was certain there was no one in. The curtains were open, and he had circled the property, peering through all the windows and checking the doors. Everything was in order. Now, Robbie walked down the High Street, pausing briefly outside Cooper's, the Estate Agents. *Maybe I should be looking for somewhere else to live. I'm not sure that I could afford any of these, though. Prices seem to have skyrocketed in Shepton Rise. Am I too old to be still living with my dad? It might have been different if Mum was still alive or if I had a girlfriend.* There was fellow police officer he was fond of, Laura, but he had never even asked her out on a date and didn't know if she already had a boyfriend. *Anyway, Dad and I get along just fine, so why change things? We support each other; we are a team. Also, I have to admit, it's great to come home to a home-cooked meal on the table. I wonder what we've got tonight? Shepherd's Pie, I hope. Still, enough of this daydreaming.*

Robbie approached the door to the left of the estate agents. He put on his latex gloves, not because it was yet another chilly day, but because he knew it was good practice. It wouldn't be helpful to leave his fingerprints all over everything. He rang the bell and waited for a voice from the intercom. It didn't come, so he tried the handle, and the door opened. Apparently it wasn't one of those sophisticated entry systems where the occupants could buzz the door open from upstairs. It would be unlocked at the start of the working day and locked again at the end. *This is promising. He must be in. The sooner I'm finished, the sooner I'll be sitting with my feet up, a cup of tea, and a honey flapjack from Heavenly Delights. I can't recall ever having met Mr Smith, but I vaguely thought my dad knew him.*

The first-floor office door was ajar.

'Hello, Mr Smith. I'm DC Broome, 'I'm here because your brother is worried about you.' Robbie used his foot to push open the office door. 'Oh!' he sighed, deflated because the room appeared empty. It looked like a meeting was in progress because the accountant had spread documents and piles of receipts on the desk, alongside two half-empty glasses of water. Before continuing his search upstairs, Robbie bent down to pick up a receipt that had fallen on the floor. It was then that he encountered Graham Smith for the first time.

***

'Sarge?'

'What do you want?'

'I've found Graham Smith, Sir.'

'Have you now. Couldn't you just put it into your report tomorrow? What's he got to say for himself?'

'Not a lot. He's been murdered.'

'Blast! I was just about to knock off. Secure the site, and I'll be over as soon as I can.'

Robbie made a second phone call.

'Dad, It looks like it's going to be a late one tonight. I'm actually in Shepton Rise, but I will have to go back to the station later and make a report. I don't suppose you could pack an overnight bag for me? I'll kip down in an empty cell because I'm on an early shift tomorrow. And, please, can you bring me a sandwich and some coffee? I can't leave this doorway. I'm outside Abacus Accountants. Someone has killed Graham Smith.'

Robbie heard noises from inside. He burst through the door to find a startled young lady standing in a doorway he hadn't noticed before, and which led through from the hallway to the estate agents.

'Excuse me, Miss. I'm DC Broome. Can you tell me what you are doing here?'

The young girl pointed nervously towards the back door, 'I've just put some rubbish in the wheelie bin outside.'

'Was that door locked?' Robbie asked.

'Yes. Sometimes Mr Smith forgets to lock and bolt it, but we always do.' Robbie could see a large key in the mortice lock and sturdy bolts, top and bottom.

'Have you seen Mr Smith lately?'

'Not for a few days. It was Thursday morning, I think. Mr Smith told me he was going to Cornwall. I expect he's still there.'

'Please, can I ask you to go back into the estate agents and lock this door behind you? Also, we will need to question all Coopers' staff who have been working here since Thursday. It would be useful if you could prepare a list for us.'

'Well, that's easy. It's just me - I'm Jodie - Kelly, and Mr Cooper.'

Robbie noted down the names and returned to his position outside the street door. *That could have been a bit awkward for me if the Sarge had encountered her there after he told me to secure the crime scene. I should have noticed that doorway. Any excuse to put me down, and you can guarantee that Bristow will seize it. I'll have to be more careful. I'm looking forward to getting stuck into this case. I wonder if there has been any animosity between Cooper and Smith. A neighbourhood dispute, so to speak.*

As Robbie waited for his father to bring his overnight bag, he noticed a CCTV camera outside Rapid Tools, the hardware shop opposite. He dialled the number displayed on the shop sign.

'Hello. I'm DC Broome. I was just wondering if your CCTV is working. This is just a heads-up that we may need to have a look at it. Who should we contact? Thanks. We'll be in touch.'

***

The following day, just as Robbie feared, his boss took over the operation and consigned Robbie to a subordinate role, mostly in charge of taking notes. A detective visited Rapid Tools and requisitioned all the CCTV footage since the previous Thursday. Robbie was pleased that he wouldn't have to trawl through that lot!

The day ended with a team briefing in the incident room, fronted by Detective Inspector Williams with Bristow at his side. If Robbie had hoped for any praise for finding the body and his subsequent actions, it wasn't forthcoming.

'Graham Smith, an accountant, has almost certainly died by strangulation,' reported Bristow, 'We can't confirm an accurate time of death yet. The last entry in Smith's diary was Thursday.' Robbie thought he detected a strange expression on Bristow's face as his boss fleetingly looked in his direction, but it quickly passed. 'Also, one of the girls in the estate agents spoke to him on Thursday. We know he was supposed to travel to Cornwall on Friday to visit his brother and didn't arrive.'

'How are you getting on with the CCTV?' asked the DI.

'They are still at it, Sir,' replied Bristow, 'There are two of them on it. Treadwell is going back in time from yesterday, and Jones is going forward from Thursday.'

'Okay. Carry on, Sergeant.'

Bristow continued. 'Now we come to suspects. We don't have any. The estate agents have easy access, although so does anyone coming in from the street, for that matter. They could have got up to his office unobserved, but it's unlikely to be one of the estate agents. Possible, but not likely. Cooper is disabled - a wheelchair user. There's no lift, so he wouldn't be able to get upstairs, never mind stand up to strangle someone. As for the two girls he employs, they are both very slight. I know better than to say on the record, with all the feminism stuff we have to put up with, that they couldn't have done it, but I doubt it, all the same. It's not as though some implement was used;

there is bruising present from the pressure of the murderer's fingers.'

'So,' the DI sighed, 'To sum up. One, we don't have a suspect; two, a motive; or three, someone with the opportunity to carry out the crime. I want a quick result on this. My boss is breathing down my neck. Get on with it.' As the DI left the room, Bristow barked out orders to his team.

'A suspect, a motive, an opportunity. Get to work and find me at least one of those. After all, as the song goes, *One out of three ain't bad*. Even though most of them were not born when the song was a hit, everyone in the room knew it should have been *Two out of three*, but no one was inclined to point it out.

***

'You wanted to see me, Sir,' said Robbie nervously. He was always worried when he was in the Chief's office.

'Yes, DC Broome. I'm afraid you are no longer on the case. We have a list of traffic infringements for you to deal with, but, for reasons I will explain, you can no longer be part of the operation. Take a seat.'

15

Monday

"Into the evening, low pressure persists, bringing wind and rain. Tomorrow will stay unseasonably cool with no long sunny periods."

***

At the same time that Robbie met with the Chief, Ginny was just about to start preparing her evening meal. She heard the doorbell ring, followed by a loud knocking.

'Alright, alright!' she murmured, 'No need for that.

I'm not deaf!' She opened the door, expecting to find a youth with a dubious identity badge and a large holdall trying to sell dishcloths and dusters to her. Or perhaps there would be a man with a white van purporting to have driven from Grimsby with a load of fresh fish. Then again, it could be a salesman from a double-glazing company, who just happened to be in the area, and who could offer her a free survey on replacement windows. Instead, she was surprised to see three uniformed police officers on her doorstep.

'Mrs Virginia Fellows?' enquired the young female officer. Ginny nodded.

'My name is PC Laura Treadmore. We would like you to come to the station to answer some questions regarding a serious crime. You are not under arrest, but I have to tell you that you have the right to remain silent. You do not have to say anything, but anything you do say may be given in evidence...'

***

Detective Inspector Williams called Bristow into his office.

'An update, please, Bristow.'

'We are holding our two suspects, Virginia Fellows and Adam Broome, ready for questioning, Sir. I'm just waiting for DC Cassidy to arrive.'

'He's the officer who has swapped duties with DC Robbie Broome, isn't he?' asked the DI.

'That's right, Sir, from City Central Station, so we won't have young Broome hindering or compromising our investigation.'

'And what have we learned from the CCTV?

'We see Fellows and Broome entering the premises last Thursday at fifteen hundred hours and departing thirty minutes later. After that, not a soul goes through that door until DC Broome on Monday. Both suspects' prints are on the water glasses on the desk, and the paperwork on it pertains to Fellows.'

'And the time of death?'

'Thursday afternoon.'

'Motive?'

'I don't know at the moment. I hope we will arrive at one through the interview, Sir.'

'Good work, Bristow.'

'Thank you, Sir.'

***

A tall young police officer walked briskly but confidently into the operations room at City Central. The hint of a smile suggested that he knew he was good-looking and destined to go places.

'Sir, I'm DC Cassidy. Sorry, I'm late, Sir. It took

me longer than I thought it would to get across the city. I would have set off sooner, but I wanted to tie up this line of enquiry. Take a look, Sir. It makes for some interesting reading.' DC Tony Cassidy handed Bristow a sheaf of papers. The Sergeant leafed through them, his lips curling into a smile as he read.

'Excellent! We'll start with Adam Broome, then. Well done Cassidy.'

Fifteen minutes later, the tape was recording, and Adam sat alongside Price, the duty solicitor, in Interview Room One, facing DC Cassidy and DS Bristow, with no idea why he had been detained.

'Does Robbie know I'm here?' he asked. Although Adam had never spoken with Detective Sergeant Bristow before, he had heard a lot about him from his son and imagined he would not be a man he could warm to.

'Detective Constable Broome has been temporarily relocated to the City Central Police Station and is no longer involved with this case, nor will he be a topic of conversation going forward,' replied Bristow.

'But what case?' asked Adam in exasperation.

'It's me who asks the questions, not you! Now, Adam Broome. Tell me about your whereabouts last Thursday afternoon.'

'Erm, I called around to my friend Ginny's house after lunch, and we had a bit of a chat. Then I went with her to Abacus Accountants. After that, we went for a coffee at Nurtures, the Garden Centre cafe. I drove Ginny home and went home myself. I cooked dinner for Robbie and me and spent the rest of the evening on the computer.'

'I'd like to return to your visit to the accountant's. What time did you get there?' asked Bristow.

'Just before three. Ginny had a three o'clock appointment.'

'And how did you find Mr Smith?' asked Bristow.

'Oh! Same as usual. He's hardly full of life, is he?'

'I couldn't possibly comment, Sir. And how did your meeting end?'

'We left him looking at Ginny's spreadsheets.'

'Did you now,' commented Bristow, looking down at the papers that Cassidy had given him. 'You knew Graham Smith from before, didn't you?'

'Yes, that's right, well it was more his father, really.'

'From your time as a travel agent?' prompted Bristow.

'That's right,' replied Adam, surprised that Bristow should know about his former occupation.

'Did you like being a travel agent?'

'Oh yes. I absolutely loved it!'

'But it was a business that ultimately went bust.'

Adam frowned. 'I wouldn't put it like that; I chose to wind the company up.'

'A business that went under, with considerable debts and under an investigation for tax evasion,' persisted Bristow.

'I wasn't evading tax. It was a simple accounting error.'

'So you were happy at having to pay back thousands of pounds in taxes and fines.'

'Well, no, of course not.'

'And your accountants were...?'

'Smith, Smith & Smith.'

'So this is how I read it, Mr Broome. You had a job that meant the world to you, but it was taken away from you by the incompetence of your accountants, and then when you went there with your friend, something snapped and, motivated by revenge, you attacked and killed Graham Smith.'

'Graham Smith is dead? I don't believe it!'

'Very convincing, Mr Broome. I hear you've been spending a lot of time with actors - you deserve an Oscar!'

'But that's ridiculous! I wound the company up because of the change in how the public booked holidays. They were doing it themselves online. And as for the accountants, it was an error. Graham's father was getting on a bit, and he made an honest mistake.'

'Mistakes cost lives,' commented Bristow drily.

***

The duty officer returned Adam to his cell. 'Time for a coffee, Cassidy,' said Bristow, ' I'll get one of the PCs to show you where everything is.' They entered the main, open-plan office, 'Treadwell!' shouted Bristow, 'This is DC Cassidy. Look after him. I'm going for a brew.' He walked away nodding in satisfaction. *He's only been here five minutes and already made his mark. He's playing a proper supporting role, not like DC Broome with all his namby-pamby, small-town meddling.*

'DC Cassidy, hello,' said Laura, 'Actually, it's Treadmore. He never gets my name right.'

'Pleased to meet you,' smiled Cassidy, 'I've been having a good day so far, and it's just got even better!'

'Oh, you charmer!' said Laura, blushing.

'Perhaps we could meet up for a drink after our shifts.'

'Well, you never know!'

***

'This one's a weird one,' said the duty officer, sliding back the viewing hatch of Ginny's cell. 'She's not moved since she got here. Just sat on the floor, staring into space.'

'There is not a lot of colour in her face. She looks like a ghost,' replied Laura. 'Anyway, Bristow has sent me to fetch her for an interview.' She lowered her voice to a whisper. 'He even said I should sit in to make her more at ease, so he can catch her out. I'm not allowed to say anything, though.'

'Virginia Fellows. Virginia Fellows!' So deep was Ginny in her meditation that the duty officer had to repeat her name several times before she realised she wasn't alone. Laura had encountered prisoners who were abusive or prone to try and escape, but this one was neither of these and walked meekly alongside her, breathing slowly and deeply. Once in the interview room, Laura sat at the back whilst Ginny faced Bristow, her eyes closed and beads of sweat forming across her forehead and upper lip. Laura noticed Bristow had taken the opportunity to wink at Cassidy. He evidently thought the condition of this suspect was tantamount to an expression of guilt.

Bristow cautioned Ginny and informed her this was a voluntary police interview.

'In that case, if it's voluntary, I should be free to leave at any time.' Price, the duty solicitor, nodded.

'That's true,' agreed Bristow, 'In which case, I would have no alternative other than to arrest you, and detain you in custody.'

'Arrest! What for?' cried Ginny in alarm.

'I was going to come on to that,' sneered Bristow, 'If you hadn't interrupted me. We have questions regarding the murder of Graham Smith on Thursday.'

'Graham Smith! But I saw him on Thursday!'

'We know that. We have strong reason to believe that Adam Broome strangled Graham Smith and that you were, at the very least, a witness to the event.'

'No, no, no, no!' Laura could see that whatever composure Fellows possessed was deserting her. She began to sway violently, then suddenly scraped her chair backwards so she could bend over with her head between her knees. Bristow carried on regardless.

'If you give us a full confession now, I'm sure it will go in your favour.'

Laura was becoming deeply worried about the suspect.

'Sarge,' she said. Bristow ploughed on; he was in full flow now.

'There's no point trying to protect him. You

should be trying to save yourself...'

'Sarge! Sarge!' Laura interrupted, 'She doesn't look well. I think we need the Medic.'

'What?' thundered Bristow. Initially, he was annoyed that the PC had the audacity to interrupt him, but he quickly realised that, as the interview was being recorded, he had no option other than to halt it. If he ignored the PC's concerns, the tape could be used as evidence against him should the suspect raise a complaint.

Later, once Virginia Fellows was in the Medic's care, Laura returned to her desk. Cassidy came over to her.

'It's a pity that you had to jump in there,' he said, 'We almost had her.' Laura didn't know what else to do other than nod. 'Anyway, how about that drink tonight? I bet you could show me some lively places to go. I'm in your hands.' He laughed, 'Hopefully!'

'I'm sorry,' replied Laura, 'My boyfriend's taking me out for a meal tonight. Maybe another time.' Laura didn't have a boyfriend, but she had mixed feelings about Cassidy. He was confident and good-looking, with a cheeky smile and a twinkle in his eye that hinted at fun times ahead. On the other hand, he was cocky and ambitious, and she didn't trust him as far as she could throw him! She sensed danger and, to use a cliched police expression, she needed to proceed with caution.

16

Monday

For obvious reasons, Robbie was finding it hard to concentrate at City Central. Firstly, his surroundings were different. He was used to the familiarity of his own desk. It wasn't that he kept any personal mementoes or photographs on it; it was more about its position in the room. *I suppose that's what Feng Shui is all about, not that I would say that in front of Bristow. He would make me the laughing stock of the station.* But that was just a minor issue. Whilst Robbie was trawling through endless reports of stolen vehicle number plates and trying to match them with getaway vehicles in major crimes, he knew that in the City South police station, Bristow would be questioning his father and Ginny for a crime that he couldn't imagine them committing in a million years.

Robbie felt powerless and completely in the dark. He knew he was not permitted to be involved with the case, but he couldn't help having a quick look. When he logged onto Intel, he found that all details related to the case were denied to him. *Oh no! What if the computer geeks see that I've tried to gain access?* He tried to put that possibility out of his mind. *Why would they? Everyone has enough to do!*

Bristow! With my dad! Robbie usually tried not to dwell on his dislike of Bristow, and he was sure that his boss felt the same way about him. Bristow thought Robbie was a small-town country boy and didn't conform to the type of police officer he wanted in his team. To get on, you had to massage his ego, "Tell us again about that time you pulled in Johnny Fingers, Sarge," or "Come on, Skipper, I'll buy you a pint; you deserve it!" Somehow, Robbie couldn't bring himself to do this convincingly. Not everyone in the station was a career police officer, determined to climb the ladder, not caring about whose toes they stood on. By all accounts, Cassidy, whose desk he was currently occupying, was very much like that, but there were many decent officers too, and some, especially Laura, he was even fond of. One thing that rankled with Bristow, that Robbie couldn't - or wouldn't - do anything about, was that Robbie returned home every evening to the small country town of Shepton Rise. In Bristow's eyes, all police officers should embrace the fast pace, grime, noise, and colour of the city. *Not for me! It was where I was born. It gives me pride in my roots and a set of good, honest values.*

Usually, Robbie was hard-working and efficient, but not today. He had been given the most tedious and mind-numbing job to do, one that no one else wanted, and he couldn't help his mind wandering. He realised he needed help and knew where to get it.

'Hi, Steve.'

'Robbie! Have you got a day off?'

'No, I'm at work and I'll have to be quick, I don't want anyone to hear this conversation. Actually, I'm not at my usual station; I've been transferred because Ginny and my dad have been taken in for questioning. They're under suspicion of murdering Graham Smith.'

'Murder! But that's ridiculous! I wondered why there was blue police tape all over the accountant's door when I passed it earlier. I assumed there had been a break-in!'

'Anyway, I'm not allowed to get involved, but I thought they might need some support, and I naturally thought of the Dead Actors.'

'Of course. That's shocking! We'll go straight down there.'

'I wouldn't do that if I were you. You wouldn't get past the front desk. I have a name for you: Laura Treadmore. She's a PC and a friend of mine. If you mention my name, she might be able to help, but ask her to promise not to tell anyone that I suggested you ring her.'

'Rest assured, Robbie, we are on the case. I know that I was the TV cop, but I reckon that Angie would be the best person to call Laura. Murder! I just can't get my head round it!'

***

'Nah! I told you I wanna speak to Laura. I ain't speakin' to no one else. 'Course I ain't gonna tell you what it's about; I ain't bleedin' stupid!' snapped Angie in a voice that she hoped would convince the operator that she was an informant, desperate to pass on some information. Finally, a puzzled voice said:

'Hello, Trixie. This is PC Laura Treadmore. Have

we met?'

'Hello Laura,' said Angie, reverting to her normal voice, 'Actually, we haven't met before. I was pretending to be one of your snouts to get to speak to you. I'll explain why in a minute.'

'I don't actually have any snouts. I'm not sure where you get them from.' Laura giggled, 'That'll get them all talking around here.'

'I'll tell you who suggested I ring you, but please don't say his name out loud,' continued Angie, 'He was really insistant that no one should know that he contacted me.'

'Go on. I'm intrigued.'

'It was Robbie Broome'

'Oh, Robbie!' exclaimed Laura, 'Oops! Sorry! I don't think anyone else heard. 'How is he?'

'He's obviously very worried about his dad and Ginny.'

'Ginny? Oh, you mean Virginia?'

'Yes. Ginny and Adam are my friends. I was astounded to hear that you suspect them of murder. I was wondering if there is anything you can tell me.'

'I can say they haven't been charged yet, and the interviews are ongoing,' replied Laura cautiously. She paused, then continued, 'I wonder if there is anything you can tell me about Mrs Fellows' health. I was rather worried about her earlier.'

'I'm especially concerned about how Ginny's coping. You see, she suffers from panic attacks and usually never leaves the house without lots of preparation.'

'I thought something was up. I can go and check on her. The medic will have seen her by now.'

'Please, if you could. I'd be grateful if you'd let me know how she is. Please tell Ginny and Adam that the Dead Actors are thinking about them.'

'Dead Actors?' exclaimed Laura.

'Oh, it's just a name some of us call ourselves. It's a long story.'

'Okay. Nice to talk to you, Trixie.'

Angie laughed. 'That's alright, darlin'. Actually, that ain't my name at all, love! Really, I'm Angie, but Trixie is wot they call me on the street. Be lucky, girl!'

***

Ginny was sitting on the floor again. Anyone who cared to peep into her cell would have thought that she was in a trance. She was, in fact, multi-tasking. On one level, she was using the meditation techniques she practised to keep herself calm, but she was also trying to visualise every detail of the day of that fateful visit to

Abacus Accountants. When she reached the end, she paused, took a few deep breaths and started again...

'Mrs Fellows.'

...and again...yes that's it! Again...

'Mrs Fellows. Ginny...Ginny...Ginny!'

Gradually, Ginny became aware that someone was calling her name, and she opened her eyes to see a young policewoman crouching in front of her.

'Ginny, are you alright?' asked Laura.

'I've been better, but I'm much better than I was earlier. You helped call the Medic, didn't you?

'Yes, that's right. You certainly sound stronger.'

'I've found a way of dealing with my circumstances - I'm channelling it like I'm a Shaolin Monk.'

'Without the Kung Fu, I hope!'

'Ah! But you should see the battles I am having with my memory! One moment, I have it in reach, and the next, it's slipped from my grasp, but just now, I think I have the upper hand.'

'That's good,' said Laura, not really understanding. Then she whispered: 'This is a secret. The Dead Actors say hello.'

'Really! How nice! Have you a means of contacting them?' Laura nodded; she had Angie's number.

'In that case, if you wouldn't mind, could you

please pass on a message? And tell me, how is Adam?'

17

Tuesday

Angie had nearly called off her search for Wilko because she was so worried about Ginny's situation. It was Steve who persuaded her to carry on with her mission.

'You may as well be busy and make yourself useful,' he had said, 'What else are you going to do - just stay at home and mope like the rest of us? If Ginny needs you to do anything, then I'm sure between Laura and Robbie, someone will get word to you.' Angie had nodded, knowing Steve was right.

She had been tearing her hair out ten minutes earlier. Not literally, because no one could see her hair. Angie had decided to dress up as her new alter-ego, Trixie, and wear a wig. If Ginny needed her help, she would throw herself into the part. The reason for Angie's stress was a problem that visited her daily, *Where did I put my keys?* It turned out that they were in a handbag that she couldn't remember using for weeks, but must have done! *I reckon there is a wicked goblin in my house who is hiding my car keys when I need them!* As a result, when Angie turned the corner into Wilko's road, the Hammertime van was already there. She was just in time to see the passenger door close before off it went at pace. Angie had wound down her window to disperse some indescribable odours filtering up from the back of her car, and she could hear the pounding beat of rap music from a hundred yards away!

I hope we aren't going too far, thought Angie, checking her fuel gauge as the van left Shepton Rise and bumped along the winding road towards Cranthorpe. She tried to hold her nerve but failed and pulled in at a garage to fill up. There wasn't a pay-at-the-pump option, and she didn't have her purse with her. *That sneaky goblin must have hidden it!* However, it wasn't a disaster because she could pay using her phone, only to find, when she returned to the car, *Aghh!* her purse had been on the floor all along, making friends with some sweet wrappers and an empty chocolate box. 'Now where?' The van had long gone. A car pulled in next to her to fill up with petrol, so Angie approached the driver.

'Excuse me. Can you please tell me if there are any building sites around here?' The driver looked her up and down.

'Funny, love, I would never have taken you for a bricklayer!' he said in an irritatingly whiny voice, obviously pleased with his witty remark. He puffed out his chest in a self-important manner, put his hands on his hips, and proceeded to impart his extensive knowledge. 'There are several around the edges of town. You'll see the Glinton estate just before you get to Cranthorpe on the left. They are building on those fields near the river that floods every year. Would you believe it? Glinton! I bet there was a glint in the developer's eye when he got permission to build there! A left turn just after that will bring you to the Dogsthorpe site. Dog's dinner, I call it. I remember when it was a rubbish dump. Some very strange smells are coming out of the ground, and I don't hold out much hope for the gardens. The earth's full of poison! Carry on, then take a left at the traffic lights, and you'll find Orton Homes. Oughtn't have built there, I say, when I was a lad ...'

'I'm sure that will be fine, Angie cut in, losing the will to live, 'I'll try those first.'

In the event, she had to look no further than the Glinton Estate, where the Hammertime van was parked on the roadside verge. Angie smiled knowingly. She could just imagine the uproar in the local community forum about the ruts and scars the contractors had made in the grass.

Around twenty houses in various stages of development were positioned so close to each other that Angie predicted a car parking nightmare in the future as thirty or forty residents jostled for space. *Mind you, if the guy at the garage is right about this estate being built on a flood plain, they might all be travelling by kayak!*

Angie spotted a young workman unloading timber from his van.

'Excuse me, I'm looking for Wilko.' The young man looked impressed.

'Blimey! I didn't think he had it in him! He's mixing cement around the back. Just walk through that gap. You can't miss him.' Angie surveyed in horror the muddy, potholed path strewn with rocks and discarded bricks.

'To quote Kirsty MacColl: "In these shoes? I don't think so!' she smiled sweetly. 'What's your name, pet?'

'Arran, who is Kirsty MacColl?'

'She was a British singer who had hits in the Eighties and Nineties.'

'I wasn't even born in the Nineties,' protested the builder.

'Would you mind getting him, Arran love,'sighed Angie, thinking there was no point adding that Bette Midler had recorded a cover version of the song. Arran part sauntered, part swaggered as far as the corner of the building and yelled:

'Oy! Wilko. C'mere.' Another, slighter youth wearing a hoody joined him, and the two jostled each other playfully as they walked back towards Angie. From nearby, a wolf whistle reminded Angie that she was dressed as Trixie. *I don't know if I should feel flattered or affronted. I wonder if I came back wearing my normal clothes and without the wig, would I get the same response? I just wish I wasn't standing in two inches of mud.*

'Hello, you wanted to see me.' The young lad pulled down his hood to reveal a mop of red hair.'

'Oh, no. It's Gerry Wilkinson I wanted to see.'

'Me Dad? He don't work here.'

'But I saw him get in the Hammertime van

yesterday,'

'Well, he did come here yesterday 'cause I'd gone in earlier and forgot my lunch, so he brought it and then went home on the bus. He's probably at home.'

You can't miss him! thought Angie sardonically as she drove back to Shepton Rise, *I seem to be very successful at missing him! I'll call in and see if he is at home.*

This time, as she was still wearing Trixie's wig, she decided to complete her disguise by adopting a strong Birmingham accent. She had once played a Brummie in a soap opera called Tee Junction, set in a Midlands Hotel.

'Excuse me, bab, sorry to mither ya, I was hopin' to have a quick chinwag with Wilko. Is he about?'

'Wilko?' queried his wife before pausing to shout back at the tumult of warring children, 'Will you just pipe down? 'No, he likes his routine, so he goes out of the house at seven-thirty - the same as when he's working at QuickMart.' She turned to yell once more, 'Will you lot just stop it?' She gave a resigned shrug. 'He doesn't like spending time in the house. I can't think why!'

Angie returned to her car, wishing she had brought another pair of shoes for her drive home. She wasn't used to wearing high heels these days and her calves were hurting. She hadn't managed to speak to Wilko yet, but Arnold Schwarzenegger's words came to her mind: *I'll be back!*

***

It had been a glorious day; one of those days when, even though it was early evening, it seemed to be getting hotter and hotter. At last, summer had arrived!

Steve's phone pinged. It was the signal he had been waiting for, and he jumped up on a stool and blew a whistle. The doors to the Red Lion opened, Pete switched the music on full volume, and everyone in the pub sang along to John Denver, only with adapted words.

'Almost heaven, Shepton Rise

Hills and valleys, clear blue skies

Life is simple; where the Red Lion stands

Friendly faces, lending hands.'

Ginny skipped into the pub, her arm linking Adam's and a broad grin on her face.

'Welcome home, Ginny,' roared Steve, echoed by others around the room.

'They had no choice, really, other than to let us go,' explained Adam later, in the snug. 'Although I took the photograph, I never gave it a second thought; it was Ginny who was brilliant enough to see the importance of it.'

'I had been going over and over the events at poor Graham Smith's,' added Ginny. 'It wasn't until I broadened my visualisations to include before and after our visit that it came to me. Adam had sent Graham a photograph via WhatsApp, and he had received a reply from him, which indicated he was alive then. The receipt from Nutures Cafe also corroborated the time, and the Rapid Tools CCTV camera confirmed that we did not re-enter the accountant's.'

'Why didn't the police spot the message on the phone when they searched the office?' asked Julia.

'Robbie told me they didn't find Graham's phone,' answered Adam.

'So, wait a minute,' said Julia, 'You could have killed Graham, stolen his phone, taken it to the cafe, then sent a message to it and answered it yourself!'

'Ha ha! Whose side are you on?' laughed Adam. 'No, they can track GPS signals using triangulation, so they know somebody, presumably the murderer, sent the reply from Graham's building.'

'So that's that. We don't know who killed Graham Smith, but we can draw a line under it now,' said Angie.

'Not so fast!' exclaimed Ginny. 'I've got a stake in this now. If you think I'm stopping there, then you've got another think coming!'

***

'Hello, is that Stephen Smith.'

'Yes. Can I help?'

'My name is Ginny Fellows, and I live in Shepton Rise. First of all, can I say how truly sorry and shocked I was to hear about your brother's murder?'

'Thank you. Fellows? I've heard that name before. Have we met?'

'No, your brother was my accountant for only a few years after I transferred my business from my London accountant. You had already left for Cornwall by then. However, you may have heard about me in connection with Graham's death because, up until today, the police suspected that my friend Adam and I were responsible, but I can assure you that we had nothing to do with it.'

'Ah, yes! That was it. The police mentioned your name.'

'Adam and I were probably the last people to see your brother alive, apart from the murderer, which has a bearing on why I'm ringing. You see, Adam took a lovely photograph of your brother in his office, and we wondered if you would like a copy.'

'I would, thank you very much. How kind,' replied

Stephen.

'Also, as I'm going to need a new accountant, I wondered how I go about getting my files back. I believe they are still spread all over your brother's desk.'

'I'm coming back to Shepton Rise next week,' said Stephen. 'Now, it's completely up to you, no pressure, but I've decided to return permanently. I'm in the process of transferring my business down here in Cornwall to another company, and I will keep the Abacus name going in Shepton Rise. So, if you like, you could be my first appointment.'

'That will be splendid. I'll bring Adam along, too; he can print the photo out for you.'

***

Ginny had one more phone call to make before she headed for bed.

'Robbie, thanks again for what you did to get Adam and me back home.'

'No worries, Ginny. It was either that or baking a cake with a hacksaw hidden inside. But, given that my Dad does all the cooking, it would probably have ended up so hard that you would need another hacksaw to get it out!'

'I've been thinking about poor Lenny. It's high

time we tried to get him free, too. I wonder if there might be anything in his room that would prove he was at the races. Do you think you could get word to him? Tell him we would like to help and ask if we could have a key to his flat. Adam knows where he lives.'

'Leave it with me, Ginny.'

'Are you back at the City South Police Station now?'

'I am, but Cassidy, the DC from City Central, is still here. The Sarge likes him. So, the dynamics have changed. Bristow always chooses him to accompany him rather than me. Even when I go for lunch, it will be me, Laura, and Cassidy now. He tends to dominate the conversation - he's good at self-promotion, if you know what I mean, and he's quicker to a joke than me - he knows how to make Laura laugh, although it's often at my expense.'

'Never mind, Robbie. You're a good lad. Anyone can see that, and I'm sure Laura will too,' said Ginny, thinking after the call ended, *but I hope she doesn't hurt you first!*

18

Wednesday

Angie realised that having a chat with Wilko in his own home might be a noisy affair - almost as loud as it had been in the Red Lion the previous night at the celebration of Adam and Ginny's return to freedom. Now, unencumbered by any worries about Ginny but hampered by a thumping headache caused by one drink too many, Angie decided it would be better to follow Wilko and have a conversation in quieter surroundings. So now she was back in the road where he lived and crawling along in her car, keeping Wilko in her sights ahead with his distinctive John Wayne-like walk,

'A man's gotta do what a man's gotta do,' drawled Angie, 'if you wanna stop at eight kids!' Wilko stopped, and so did Angie. Then, the sudden blast of a horn sent Angie's headache to the next level. A bus was behind her, and it couldn't get past because of the parked cars on the other side of the road. Angie drove further down the street. When she pulled in and looked in her mirror, she saw Wilko standing at a bus stop. She watched him board the bus, which overtook her, so once again Angie was trailing a vehicle, and once again, she was heading for Cranthorpe. The bus turned right just after the Glinton Estate. No one had got off the bus, so Wilko wasn't on another sandwich drop. They passed the "Dog's Dinner" estate, which was a hotch-potch of architectural styles, from Mock-Tudor to Colonial to imitation Barn-Conversion.

Angie got stuck at a set of traffic lights and watched with dismay as Wilko alighted from the bus and walked down a side road. When she finally reached the spot, Angie found it was a one-way street, so she had to turn down the next street and double back. *Wouldn't you believe it! He's gone!* Angie was despondent. She didn't want to give up, but she could hardly knock on every house door looking for him. She stopped outside a small recreation ground and resigned herself to spending thirty minutes reading and deleting emails on her phone, so at least she would have something to show for the morning. However, after a few minutes, she saw a man walking towards her, holding the hand of a small girl, while three other children skipped on ahead. As they drew closer, it dawned on Angie that all three children had red hair, the same as Wilko's! *Oh no! He must have a wife and family in each town! I wonder if they know about each other? I can't cope with this now!*

***

Ginny had decided that the best way to embrace her freedom was to return to doing normal things - in short, to get back to work. However, the real challenge was deciding what to prioritise. The murder case had countless unexplored avenues, leaving her feeling lost. Ultimately, her 'real job' took precedence when her phone rang.

'Hello Ginny, it's Beatrice.'

'Beatrice! Long time no see. I don't think we've spoken since I left London.'

'You are right. It's been forever! Ginny, I'm casting *Fiddler on the Roof* and we are looking for an understudy for Golde, the mother. I believe you have an actress on your books who I saw in a production of

Rose Colored Glass, the Sue Bigelow and Janice Goldberg play. I remember she captured the essence of a Jewish matriarch with great sensitivity and without resorting to caricature. Can she sing? Do you think she will be available from November to January?'

'That was Julia Grey. Yes, she has a very strong voice, and she may well have an opening then. I will ask her. In the meantime, shall I ping you over her Spotlight profile?'

'That will be great, Ginny. So, what's it like living out in the sticks? Remind me where you are again.'

'I'm in a pretty, small town called Shepton Rise. It's where I grew up, and it's almost as though the town has folded itself around me to support me.'

'Oh, that's lovely; I was shocked to hear about your poor husband, so I'm glad things are working out for you now. Shepton Rise... Shepton Rise. I'm sure I've heard of it before. Never mind, it will come to me, eventually. Anyway, send me that CV, and I promise I won't leave it so long before I ring again.'

***

Denny was already at Nurtures Cafe when Adam breezed in, a spring in his step.

'Well, well, well! It's the jailbird. How's it going, Adam!' laughed Denny.

'Ha! It's good to be breathing the sweet smell of freedom.'

'I'm happy to be inhaling this aroma of good coffee,' commented Denny.

'How's the project going?' asked Adam.

'Mostly okay. I've not discovered anything criminal. Nor is there any evidence that a sinister foreign power has infiltrated the Town Hall computers, which has to be a good thing.'

'You said, "mostly"!'

'I need to dig a little deeper into the public access computers, such as the ones in the Library,' said Denny.

'Actually, I've just come from there. I've been spending a lot of time on the Library computers,' said Adam, 'My laptop at home is running very slow.'

'Tell me about it! Aren't we all these days?' smiled Denny.

***

On the edge of town lies a small row of Victorian terraced houses, their red brick facades contrasting sharply with the honeyed limestone of the historic centre. A perpetual topic of conversation among the residents of these homes is the view, not one of breathtaking beauty but quite the opposite. Back in the 1960s, the Town Council, who were more concerned with the problem of housing low-income families than creating an aesthetic legacy, approved the construction of a two-storey concrete building comprising twelve one and two-bedroom apartments. The front doors, painted a uniform bottle green, line the external, covered balconies, and had the residents of the terraced houses twitched aside their net curtains to tut-tut at the goings on, they might have noticed two people walking along the top landing searching for number Eight, The Cedars.

'Here we are,' said Doc, 'You get a nice view from here - that Victorian terrace is pretty, isn't it? In what dastardly, ingenious place did Ginny say that Lenny had hidden the key?' Julia bent down and picked up a terracotta pot that had once been home to a house plant, but the petrified remains gave no clue as to what species it might have been.

Julia held up a set of keys. 'Right here. Such an obvious place that no one would ever think to look there! It's lucky for us that Lenny never went out with his keys in his pocket. He had lost them in pubs once too often, apparently. If the police had impounded his only set, it would have created an awful lot of paperwork to get them back.'

'Here we go, then,' said Doc, turning the key in the

lock and opening the door. 'Ugh!' he gasped.

'I think I'll use this pot to prop the door open. What's the difference between musty and fusty? It's all rolled into one in there - it smells like a time capsule, somewhere that's not encountered any fresh air since 1973! After you!'

'No, after you!'

'I insist, after you!'

They stepped into Lenny's apartment and stood for a moment to take stock of. It wasn't hard to identify Lenny's favourite pastime. Armed with nothing more than a pair of scissors, a box of drawing pins, several copies of the Racing Times and an assortment of tabloid newspapers, Lenny had covered the walls of his living room with photographs of racehorses, creating a patchwork of sepia and faded yellow.

'Some of these are really old,' marvelled Doc, 'Look, here's a photo of Shergar!'

'That's that horse that was kidnapped and never found isn't it? Don't tell me Lenny's responsible!'

'We had better be careful when we go in the bedroom,' said Doc. 'If Shergar's in there, he's going to be one grumpy stallion after all this time!'

In the event, there was nothing of interest in the lounge or the small kitchen, nor was there a racehorse in the bedroom waiting for his moment to bolt for freedom.

'Robbie told us there was a load of cash on this bedside cabinet, which the police have confiscated,' said Julia. Doc walked over and peered behind it.

'Hmm!' he murmured, 'There's a certain amount of debris behind here. Against my better judgement, I suppose I ought to take a closer look.' Doc pulled the cabinet away from the wall, revealing a pile of receipts and notes covered in dust and fluff. Doc gingerly lifted a folded piece of paper from the top of the pile. He flattened it out, and they both studied it.

'What is that?' asked Julia.

'I do believe it's what is called an accumulator bet with the Tote. Who knows if the horses listed here won, but what's important is that it was bought at a specific racecourse on a specific day at a specific time. It's an alibi! Erm, do you think I need to delve into that lot?' Doc grimaced at the remaining pile of rubbish, 'Goodness knows what is lurking in there - Gollum maybe, or Stig of the Dump, or perhaps a new virus, resistant to antibiotics?'

'No, that would be above and beyond the call of duty!' laughed Julia. 'Come on, let's show this to Ginny.'

***

'Excellent news!' said Ginny with a smile. 'Not only does the Tote betting slip prove that Lenny was where he said he was, but I've phoned the Tote, and guess what? He won! Lenny has over three thousand pounds coming to him.' Ginny beamed as all the Dead Actors cheered, then, alerted by a notification, she looked at her phone. 'It's from Rupert!' Ginny opened the photo Julia's son had sent, clapped her hands with delight, and passed her phone around so the others could see. It was a screenshot Rupert had discovered on someone's Facebook account, and it featured a selfie taken by a young girl. In the background was a racecourse grandstand, and in the foreground, flanking the girl, were Ricky Flynn, smiling but looking slightly the worse for wear, and Lenny Peters, who appeared bemused, or perhaps confused, by someone wanting to take his photograph.

Ginny's phone rang.

'So sorry, I should have turned it to silent,' she said, but then, glancing at the caller's name, announced, 'I'd better take this. It may be about work for one of you.' She picked up her phone, and as she left the room, the Dead Actors heard her say, 'Beatrice! You said you wouldn't leave it so long before you rang...'

'I don't know about you,' said Angie. 'Considering I'm between gigs, I don't think I've ever been so busy.' Just then, Ginny returned to the room, holding her phone aloft.

'It's Beatrice Kent; some of you may know her as a Casting Director, but I'm afraid it's not about work. Beatrice started to tell me something interesting, but I stopped her and asked if I could put her on loudspeaker so you could all hear.' Ginny placed the phone on the table.

'Hello all! I'm not used to being the one facing an audience! I was speaking to Ginny this morning, and I couldn't think why the name Shepton Rise was familiar. It came to me a few moments ago, so I thought I would ring. Last year, I was approached by the director of an amateur theatre group based in Shepton Rise who was hoping I had something suitable for him. His name was Matthew Walker, and I actually acted in one of his productions when I was at University before I realised that my talents lay elsewhere, as you are probably realising.'

'No, no, carry on!' came a chorus from the room.'

'I couldn't help him, but out of interest, I searched for the theatre company on the Internet; I wanted to see if I had aged better than he had.'

'I'm sure you had,' interjected Ginny.

'Anyway, I had a production of *Jersey Boys* coming up and one of the other Stage Centre actors, Jack something or other, was a dead ringer for Frankie Valli, so I emailed Matthew asking him if he could ask Jack to get in touch to come for an audition. Well, I didn't hear anything, but by then, I was on a mission! I looked at some publicity material and noticed that Jack's name appeared to be connected to a butcher who was a sponsor.'

'Was it Jack Knight? His butcher's shop is called Prime Cuts,' Julia called out.

'Yes, that's him. So, I sent Jack an email and then, would you believe it, half an hour later, I got an email from Matthew explaining that Jack didn't have a very good singing voice and, in any case, he was tied up with one of his own productions. Anyway, I thought no more about it until Jack rang me himself. It seemed that Matthew hadn't passed on my message, and when I tried to suggest tactfully that, according to Matthew, a singing role might not be the best fit, he just exploded. He was yelling so loudly I had to hold the phone away from my ear, and I never realised there were so many places to insert a four-letter word into one sentence! After that rant, I decided we wouldn't want anybody so volatile in the company and I left the matter there. So that's my Shepton Rise story. As it happened, there was some problem with the rights, so the producers didn't put the musical on anyway. Hope that helps, Ginny, I'll be back in touch soon about that other thing. Bye for now.'

Steve punched the air. 'Bye, Bye, Baby! That means not only do we have the evidence to free Lenny, but we now have a motive for Jack! Oh, what a night!'

'This calls for a toast, Ginny. Have you got any sherry?' asked Doc.

'I won't be upset if you haven't. Big girls don't cry!' added Angie

'Here's your phone, Ginny', said Julia, passing it to Steve next to her, 'It's working its way back to you.'

'Thank you, everyone,' said Ginny, 'This is a night to remember!'

19

Thursday

Angie was in the Cozy Corner Cafe, which ironically wasn't on a corner but sandwiched between Prime Cuts and QuickMart, stirring her coffee for much longer than necessary, seeing that she drank it black without sugar. Whilst she was happy to learn that Ginny was still focused on finding the truth about the murders, she had unresolved matters of her own to worry about. At one point during last night's meeting, Steve had glanced at her and raised an eyebrow as if to ask, 'Are you going to mention that you've been tailing

Wilko?' but she had shaken her head. She didn't have anything positive to report. Not only that, she had a dilemma. Should she say anything about Wilko's other family? Of course, it would only be a criminal offence if he was married to two women. Eleven children! A voice interrupted her thoughts.

'Excuse me, love. Do you mind if I sit here? These are the last free seats in the cafe, and I've arranged to meet my wife here shortly.'

'Of course,' said Angie, then as she looked up and met his eyes, her heart skipped a beat. Angie had never heard him speak before, nor, she realised, had Wilko ever seen her before.

'Ow, ooh, ow!' Wilko winced as he lowered himself into his seat, 'Here she is now.'

'Oh, hello love, so you found him.'

'Found him?' queried Wilko.

'This lady was looking for you. I must say, you look better without that wig.'

'Found me?' asked Wilko.

'So you knew it was me?' Angie asked.

'Oh yes. I mean, you do a good job disguising yourself with a Brummie accent, and it was a very good wig, but it was your nails that gave it away.'

'My nails!' Angie inspected her nails and realised

how badly she needed a manicure.

'What do you mean, found me?' implored Wilko. His wife continued to ignore him.

'I notice these things. My name's Jean, by the way. I used to work in a nail bar. I still have a few private clients but can only see them when the kids are in school or at the nursery. Or, like today, when they are at his sister's.'

'His sister's?' asked Angie.

'Yes, in Cranthorpe. There's a park just near their house. We take turns. Once a week our kids go there, then the next week I look after them all. Although, yesterday he went on his own to babysit for a few hours,' explained Jean.

Angie smiled. *Thank goodness that's the mystery solved!* 'Actually, I didn't find him; he found me,' she said, turning to Wilko.

'How did I find you?' he asked exasperated.

'I did want to ask you something,' said Angie. 'It's about your old boss, Matthew Walker. I wondered if you knew anyone who might have had a grudge against him?'

'Well, obviously, Lenny and he didn't get along.' Wilko paused, scratching his chin while he thought. 'There was one strange thing that happened once.'

'Go on!'

'It was a few weeks ago. Jack, the butcher from Prime Cuts, stormed in and demanded to see Matthew. Well, as it happened, he'd gone to the dentist, so Elsie was covering. I don't know what he wanted, but there he was, in his stripy apron, all covered in blood, and he was holding a meat cleaver, and he was so angry that he threw it against the wall so hard that it stuck in. I'll give him his due, though. He came back later with some filler and repaired the gash he had made. He's got a temper, that one!'

***

Ginny and Adam had timed it so they would be early for the appointment with Stephen Smith. It helped Ginny stay calm if she didn't have to rush, and in any case, she hated being late. Knowing how hard it could be to park on the High Street, Adam was only too pleased to set off early and even happier to find a spot only a few yards from the accountants. First though, he had to wait while a bright pink VW camper van manoeuvred into a space.

'Nice!' Adam commented, 'It's an early one. You can tell by the split front windscreen. 1960s I reckon.' Ginny nodded distractedly, more concerned about her own private battle. While it was one thing conquering her fears about leaving the house, it was quite another returning to the scene of a murder.

Adam and Ginny arrived at the door to Abacus Accountants at the same time as the camper van driver. He was a tall man in his sixties with a long silver ponytail, and a string of beads around his neck. It was quite obvious to Ginny and Adam who he was because on the front of his black T-shirt was emblazoned a colourful surfboard about to be engulfed by a giant wave.

'Mr Smith?' ventured Ginny.

'Hi, Yes, sorry. Call me Stephen. I meant to get here before you,' he replied, shaking hands with Ginny and Adam. 'I got held up on the motorway and Rhonda didn't help. I didn't even have time to get changed.' Stephen gestured towards the camper van. 'That's Rhonda. A good old girl, but there's no hurrying her.'

'I know just how she feels,' laughed Ginny.

'I'm a bit apprehensive about what I'm going to find here, to be honest,' said Stephen, peeling away blue police tape stuck to the door frame.

Ginny and Adam followed Stephen upstairs and paused on the threshold of Graham's office to take in the scene. Ginny's files were still spread out on the desk. There was no sign that a murder had been committed here.

'It looks just the same as it did when we were last here,' observed Adam. Ginny scanned the room slowly. Something was niggling her. *The police would have noticed if anything was amiss wouldn't they?*

'Hmm! I'm not sure. Stephen, would it be alright if Adam took a couple of photos of the room?'

'Sure! I don't think I'll use this room as my office anyway. Dad's old room upstairs is bigger and has a better view.'

'Don't think you'll be able to see the sea, though,' grinned Adam.

'True, very true,' replied Stephen, sadly.

***

'It's very good of you to spend time on your day off fixing up my computer,' said Ginny, setting down a tray of tea and biscuits.

'Oh, that's okay,' replied Denny. 'I'm glad to help. I remember you from school. I doubt if you can remember me, as I was a bit of a nerd.'

'I can, actually. Weren't you in a band with Adam?'

'Yes, I'm afraid to say - a crime against music.'

'How's your project for the Town Hall going? Adam tells me you didn't find any evidence of unsavoury or criminal activities on their computer network.'

'No, that's right, although I did find some surprising results when I analysed the Library Computers.'

'Ooh, tell me more,' exclaimed Ginny.

'No, I shouldn't.'

'Not even if I offered you another biscuit?'

'They do look rather nice...'

***

On the evening of Lenny Peters' release from prison, Pete and Emma threw a welcome party for all the locals at the Red Lion. Lenny popped in beforehand and put some of his winnings behind the bar to cover free drinks for the regulars.

'I've got this vague idea that I may have upset some tennis ladies,' Lenny admitted, 'Invite 'em along.' Pete duly did this, and they were only too happy to attend. In fact, one of them owned a quarter-share of a racehorse and gave Lenny many tips on racehorses she claimed were dead certs, but, in reality, would give Lenny ample opportunity to lose yet more money. The important point was that they held no grudges against him and even invited him to their Wimbledon Finals Parties, which they planned to hold in mid-July.

As usual, Pete put a lot of effort into his playlist,

and, as usual, most of his clientele were absolutely oblivious to it. As Lenny walked through the door, a trumpet played a refrain like a bugle reveille. It was the opening bars of the Pioneers' *Long Shot Kick de Bucket* from the 1960s. Pete had to translate the Jamaican patois for Emma.

'It's about a man losing all his money on a racehorse that dropped dead during the race - he kicked the bucket!' Charlie Dibbs, who worked at the Garden Centre, knew the song. He had been a big fan of the Two-tone Ska revival in the early eighties and jumped up and entertained the pub with his Nutty Boy dance. The song that got the best reaction was the Osmonds' *Crazy Horses*, with everyone mimicking the squealing horse sound with varying degrees of success and lots of laughter. The sight of Charlie Dibbs and Susan Cunningham-Hill from the Tennis Club leading a line dance to *The Race Is On* by George Jones was a memory that made Pete smile for the rest of the night.

Angie read out a message from Ricky Flynn. She gave it the full Hollywood Oscar ceremony treatment.

'I'm sorry that I couldn't be there today, Lenny. I'm away filming on location...'

Perched on a ledge was an abandoned, half-drunk glass of beer; its owner had left early, unable to get into the party spirit. All the references to horseracing served as a depressing reminder of a recent run of bad luck and some heavy losses.

Ginny wasn't at the Red Lion either. Until recently, she couldn't have imagined that she would be out of the house as much as she had been lately. Now, she was relishing an evening of peace and quiet with Tuxie on her lap and time to ponder and make sense of recent events. Her phone was set to silent, although she did reach for it at one point to text Adam.

'How is the party?'

'I didn't stay to the end, but everyone was having fun.'

'Good. I'm pleased for Lenny, night night.'

20

Friday

Tuxie didn't mind. She didn't mind one little bit! It was Ginny who was troubled. Tuxie closed her eyes, giving a purr of satisfaction. Ginny's eyes were shut, too, as she continued to stroke and stroke and try to make sense of the jumbled thoughts that went round and round in her head, picturing all the suspects that might be responsible for Matthew's murder. *All I know for certain is that Lenny didn't do it. Ashley or Chris might be in the frame. Just because what we had assumed was a meeting of conspirators turned out to be a planning meeting for an innocent birthday party, it didn't preclude their involvement, either individually or together. Also fully in the spotlight is Jack. Wilko's tale highlights Jack's quick temper, and Beatrice has given us a good reason why he might have sought revenge. Any aspiring actor would be cross if they learned they had been denied the opportunity to perform in the West End. But would they kill because of it? Then, to make things worse, there is the murder of poor Graham Smith.* Ginny paused momentarily as the enormity of the task ahead rose within her like a wave. Tuxie gave an impatient yowl of displeasure because Ginny had stopped stroking her.

Maybe I should put Matthew's case to one side and look at Graham's first.

'Sorry, Tuxie. I need to go into the office.' Ginny stood up, forcing the cat to jump off her lap. Tuxie swished her tail and stalked out of the open door into the garden as if to say, Charming! I know when I'm not wanted!

'At least it's a lovely evening for you, now the weather has turned,' Ginny called after her grumpy pet.

Five minutes later, Ginny was holding a mug of coffee and staring vacantly at two photographs. One was on her PC, the other on her laptop, and they both featured the same view. For a moment, Ginny had drifted off into her memories, recalling the times she had curled up in this same room, while her father added up columns of numbers in his head and she pored over the puzzles in her weekly comic, playing *Spot The Difference.*

Adam had taken both photographs of the accountant's office. There was one very obvious difference: the earlier one depicted Graham Smith standing in the foreground and looking self-conscious whereas the later one was taken after his murder. However, Ginny was more interested in what was happening in the background of the photographs. She studied them minutely and methodically. *What am I missing?*

'Aha! Fancy!' she exclaimed. *But I need some firmer evidence than this. I need a police photograph taken of the same view.* Ginny considered telephoning Robbie, but then decided she might as well contact PC Laura Treadmore directly. Laura was delighted to hear from Ginny and was relieved to hear that she had recovered from her brief period of incarceration. It didn't take Ginny long to persuade Laura to agree to send her the photograph she wanted. She stressed that she didn't want to see the body in the photograph and that she would not tell anyone that she had it. She simply wanted to reassure herself that Adam's photo accurately depicted the murder scene.

***

Ginny phoned Robbie.

'Are you back on the murder investigations now? Matthew Walker as well as Graham Smith?'

'No. They have still got me tracking down numberplates, although I am allowed to sit at my own desk at City South now.'

'Shame.'

'The Guvnor has kept Cassidy on working with Bristow.'

'Double shame. Robbie, would it be possible for you to look at the CCTV from Rapid Tools? I wondered if you could send me a screenshot of anyone who visited Abacus before your dad and me. I'm reluctant to ask Laura because I don't want her to get into trouble.'

'I appreciate that Ginny, but Laura would be best placed to do it because she already has authorisation to view the footage. I'll have to pick my moment to ask her, though, because Cassidy is always buzzing around her. He wouldn't hesitate to shop me - he would do anything to rise up the ranks.'

'Thanks, Robbie. It's a long shot, but if we could talk to anyone who visited, we might discover that they noticed something useful.'

***

'Hello, good to meet you at last, Jay,' said Julia, 'When did you get back from University?'

'I just came home yesterday,' replied the handsome young student. 'I'm keen to get cracking on the play.'

'You've got quite a lot of catching up to do, but with hard work, I'm sure you will get there.'

'Yeah, well, all the others have to work during the day, but I'll have a lot of spare time for the next few weeks. I'm back at Mum and Dad's; I don't have rent or food to pay for, so I can put off getting a job for a while.'

'Actually, I was a bit apprehensive about meeting you because in case you were covered in tattoos or had really long hair. I've decided we will make this a period piece, and set it in the 1950s.'

Jay laughed 'No tattoos. My hair was quite long until a few weeks ago. I had it cut here in Shepton Rise, actually, at 'Hair I Am'. I've been getting my hair cut there since I was a kid. I wouldn't trust any of the barbers near my Uni. It was my brother's wedding, so I needed to look smarter.'

'So you've been back recently then? Did you see Matthew?'

'No. It was the same weekend he was killed. I was going to call in to QuickMart on Sunday on my way back to the station, but it was closed.'

'I hear he was a complex character. How did you get on with him?' asked Julia.

'I don't like to speak ill of the dead, but he could be pretty mean at times. He would say some cruel things, and he didn't mind who heard him. I think he resented the fact that I'm on a drama course at Uni, whereas he did something boring like Business Studies when he was a student.'

Could Jay have done it? wondered Julia. *He was around at the right time. Maybe they did see each other, and Mathew said something nasty, so he snapped!*

'So where do we start?' asked Jay.

'Okay, you are playing the part of Clifford, a talented student.'

'No change there, then,' laughed Jay.

'And Sidney Bruhl, a failing playwright, has a grudge against you and wants to pass your work off as his own.'

'Cool!'

There are parallels with real life here. An older man jealous of a younger man, with murder on the horizon!

21

Friday

Adam was frustrated with his laptop. It was operating at a snail's pace! He could guess the kind of advice the sales assistant at *PC Heaven* would give him should he take it in for a service:

'Things have moved on, mate. This laptop is practically a relic—it belongs in a museum. You're running an outdated operating system that can no longer handle modern applications efficiently. Your RAM is severely limited, causing significant bottlenecks, and your graphics card is not capable of supporting current GPU-intensive tasks. You could try a system refresh, but in all honesty, it's like putting a band-aid on a bullet wound. You'd be much better off investing in a new model with a multi-core processor, SSD storage, and at least 16GB of RAM. You know the saying, 'You can't make a silk purse out of a sow's ear.' Though, why anyone would want to is beyond me. Anyway, take a look at these new models with the latest...' And all that would take money. Money Adam didn't have!

Adam was surprised to find the library empty. However, a computer monitor flickering at one of the workstations indicated someone had been there recently. Adam could easily have spent the day reading photography books, although it rankled that he still had a fair way to go before he could afford a decent camera. *The way things are going, I wouldn't like to bet on the possibility of buying one by Christmas!*

Adam wandered over to one of the computers, but before he could sit down, his phone sent him a notification. It wasn't anything important; it was just from a website that he had glanced at sending him an introductory offer. *They are all like that, sweeteners to suck you in, and then once they have their claws into you, they will bleed you dry!* However, it served to remind Adam that he should have turned his phone to silent, even though no one was in the library to tut and shush him. Adam glanced at the monitor in front of him. Then, two things happened almost simultaneously. Firstly, an ear-splitting ringing disorientated him, and then he felt a crashing blow to the back of his head. As he slipped into unconsciousness, he was aware of footsteps and someone shouting.

'What's happened?'

'I don't know, I just found him there.'

'We can't leave him; what if it's not a fire drill...'

Then all was darkness.

***

'How is Adam Broome, nurse?' asked Patrick.

'He may well be a little confused. It's a typical symptom of concussion. He will also probably be dizzy, so please ring for assistance if he needs to go to the bathroom. Are you a friend or relative?'

'Neither, really. I run the library in Shepton Rise, where he was found, and Mr Broome is a regular visitor. I didn't see the accident happen, but I thought I would come and see him as soon as possible. I won't keep you - I know how busy you all are. I can see him at the other end of the ward.'

'I hope someone told you that visiting hours end

in fifteen minutes.'

Patrick nodded, walked down the ward and sat on the chair next to the bed where Adam was lying with his eyes closed. From one wrist, a tube was connected to a drip suspended on a stand. What looked like a clothes peg on Adam's finger was connected to an ECG machine whose monitor displayed a steady heart rate.

'Adam,' Patrick said gently, 'Adam. How are you? It's Patrick. I've come to see you.' Adam opened his eyes slowly.

'To tell you the truth, I'm not too sure. I gather I'm in a hospital, but where?'

'You are in the City General, Adam. Do you know what happened?'

'No. I remember going into the library, but after that, I can't remember anything except flashing lights and a bell ringing. When I woke up, I was in this bed. Do you know what happened?'

'The bell you heard was a fire alarm. There was a drill, and the members of the Friday Book Club found you as they came rushing through to get to the exit. I arrived on the scene just after. Maybe you fainted, or tripped and banged your head. I called an ambulance immediately. We were all so worried about you. Luckily, the ambulance came quickly. I followed on and waited until they said I could see you. Unfortunately, visiting hours end in a few minutes. '

'Thank you, Patrick. Does anyone else know I'm here? My son Robbie, or Ginny?'

'I don't honestly know,' replied Patrick, 'I've got Ginny's number in my phone. Would she be able to tell your son?'

'Oh yes, she can tell Robbie. Please will you let her know?' whispered Adam.

'Certainly,' Patrick reassured him.

Adam, closed his eyes, 'I'm tired now. Thank you for coming.'

***

Ginny was in a panic. One minute, she was paying invoices for Stage Centre, her head filled with the cost of costume hire and printing posters, the next, after the phone call from Patrick, her day was turned upside down. *The man I care about more than any other is lying in a hospital bed!* Ginny had immediately passed the news on to Robbie, who was on duty, and he said he would contact the hospital. She had tried ringing Adam's phone, but either he was out of signal range, the battery was flat, or worse! The hospital would only communicate with relatives, and there were two other major problems. Firstly, visiting hours had finished, and secondly, Ginny knew that she was in no fit state to risk travelling to the city and braving the busy, chaotic world of a hospital ward. *I might end up in a hospital bed myself!* After a few deep breaths to calm herself down, Ginny knew what to do. *I need help, and I know just where to get it!*

***

Doc strode briskly along the corridor. A hospital like this was the environment that had been part of his life for years. Admittedly, he didn't have a camera crew tracking his every move and a script to follow. Still, the City General looked very much like the sets of *Emergency Level Red* where, as Edward Ramsey, he had saved countless lives on the small screen and eventually lost his own. Doc was familiar with the working practices of the nurses and orderlies that he passed, but he had no doubts about which role he would adopt today - consultant. Nobody would dare tell a consultant what to do; there would be no danger of being instructed to wheel a patient to the operating theatre or mop up a disagreeable puddle. All he needed was a clipboard, a name badge, and the confidence to pull it off.

'Nurse,' he said, in the clipped, educated tone of a

man assured of his authority, 'I'm looking for Adam Broome, admitted earlier today.'

'He's in the far bed, on the left, Sir,' replied the nurse, slightly surprised that the patient would be seen again so soon after he had been visited by another consultant, Ms Kovalenko, complete with a train of student doctors following in her wake. Still, it wasn't her job to question the whys and wherefores of such matters. She had enough on her plate as it was!

Doc noticed that the bed beside Adam was empty, which was good - less chance of being overheard.

'Now then, Mr Broome. Let's have a little privacy,' he said, drawing the curtains to screen the bed.

'Oh, what is it this time? More blood tests? I feel like a pin cushion!' moaned Adam as he opened his eyes. They opened even wider at the sight of Doc at his bedside, finger on lips.

'Hello, Adam,' said Doc quietly. 'Ginny sends her regards. Obviously, in my role as a senior consultant, I couldn't bring you a gift, so I drew you this.' Doc produced a piece of paper from beneath the official-looking notes on his clipboard, on which he had drawn a bunch of grapes and a posy of flowers, demonstrating that his artistic prowess had hardly developed since the age of seven.

'That's sweet of you. Patrick kindly said he would let Ginny know where I was. A nurse gave me a message that Robbie will be coming tonight. Unfortunately, my phone is dead.'

'Ah! One other thing I could bring you is this,' Doc said, delving into his jacket pocket and pulling out a charging lead and a plug, 'Ginny said you might need it.'

'She is a star! How is she?'

'Very worried but calmer once she knew I was coming to see you. What happened?'

'I'm not really sure. It's all jumbled up. Patrick told me there was a fire drill, and somehow, I bumped my head. I remember voices, which I now know were the Friday Book Club, and flickering lights. For some reason, I've got an image of fruit in my mind: grapes and cherries.'

'Maybe you are psychic,' said Doc, pointing to his drawing, 'And everything was leading up to this moment.'

'If I just wanted a chat, Doc, I can think of easier ways to make it happen,' laughed Adam before grimacing and feeling the bump on his head.

'Coincidentally, I watched an episode of *Only When I Laugh* last night,' said Doc, 'Do you remember it? A sitcom set in a hospital.'

'Yes, I do. You're finding it hard to leave this life behind you, aren't you, Doc.'

'Yes, I must admit I am. I've got a penknife in my pocket. Is there anything I can remove just to keep my hand in? Gall bladder? Appendix, perhaps? You won't miss your appendix.'

Adam laughed, 'Oooh!' He rubbed his sore head again.

22

Sunday, July.

The Shepton Rise Summer Fete is always held on the recreation ground, or *The Rec*, as it is more commonly known, on the first Sunday in July. Much to the annoyance of the local football team, a large pavilion now graced what would normally be the penalty area. The players were worried that the pitch would be damaged as the local derby between the Shepton Shooters and the Cranthorpe Crazies was scheduled for the following week. Beneath the canvas, pride of place was given to a table bearing produce from the local allotment society. It looked like a matter of millimetres this year would decide the prize for the largest marrow. To settle tape-measure disputes, Old Henry had constructed a device rather like ones used for measuring feet in shoe shops, and the contest was due to be settled at two o'clock with all the drama of a heavyweight boxing match.

Another group of contestants were eyeing each other with suspicion. These ladies from the Women's Institute were the entrants in the jam-making contest, and their jars, in an array of colours from yellow through orange and red to dark purple, were lined up, ready to be judged by the Lady Mayoress.

Under a gazebo, near the area that had been sectioned off for the dog show, the Stage Centre members were praying that it wouldn't rain, for the gazebo served as their changing room. One member of the group, Patrick, had two roles. He was there to promote their next production, *Deathtrap*, but he was also handing out fliers for the impending book festival at the library. In celebration of this, Stage Centre were running a quiz. The actors were going to perform a series of charades for the audience to guess, in which they would act out lines from films and musicals that had been adapted from books. The winners would get two free tickets to Deathtrap and a bottle of champagne.

'It's harder than some might think,' said Julia to Ginny, 'They have to guess the name of the film and the book. I'm sure most people will guess *Cabaret* from the moment Angie and I come out in our bowler hats and sit on chairs the wrong way round, even before we have sung a note, but I bet you not many people will know the book was called *Goodbye to Berlin*.'

'By Christopher Isherwood,' responded Ginny.

'Don't you dare enter!' laughed Julia. 'You would probably get them all right. You don't need a ticket to see the play in any case, as you are backing it.'

Ginny was feeling quite relaxed considering she was outdoors. She couldn't have managed an appearance without the support of the Dead Actors because Adam, although on the mend, was still in hospital. Ginny was sitting on a stool near the gazebo, and she had resolved to stay on the fringes of the action, away from the crowds. Inside, things were not so calm. Jack had seen the bear costume that he was supposed to wear.

'I tell you, I am not, I repeat, not wearing that flea-bitten thing!'

'But you have to,' pleaded Ashley. 'Jay can't do it;

he's playing *Mowgli*, and Chris has had to work today!'

'You can stuff it! I'm off!' Jack kicked the offending costume, sending it skittering across the tent, and stormed off.

'Now what?' wailed Ashley.

'I'll do it,' said Patrick.

'You'll do it?' cried Ashley in surprise.

'Yes, I'll do it. I'll need to read the lines; I won't be able to memorise them, but I'll play all Jack's parts.'

In the event, his decision proved a masterstroke. The meek and self-effacing librarian's performance generated many more laughs than Jack's rumbustious style would have done.

Ginny laughed along with the audience at Patrick's efforts. She suspected that some of it was an act in itself and that he was following an age-old variety and vaudeville tradition of playing an inept performer.

Ginny jotted down the answers for her own amusement.

The *Jungle Book* was an easy one, as was the next one, which featured Patrick attempting to tap dance while singing, *Chim chiminey, chim chiminey, chim chim cher-ee.* Slightly more difficult was hearing Angie, wearing a fedora, a plum stuffed in each cheek, saying, *I'm gonna make him an offer he can't refuse.* Ginny figured that Angie was standing in for Jack. She laughed when Jay sashayed on wearing a skirt, saying, *I'll try and be what she loves to call me: a little man, and not be rough and wild, but do my duty here instead of wanting to be somewhere else.* She suspected it was deliberately intended to confuse. There was one scene that had Ginny beaten. Patrick stood before his audience, a silk scarf tied around his forehead, panting: *I want, what they want, and every other guy who came over here and spilled his guts and gave everything he had, wants! For our country to love us as much as we love it! That's what I want!* She knew the name of the character, but she couldn't remember the name of the film, and she didn't realise it was a book. She had assumed the actor had written the speech.

Afterwards, she called Julia over and held out her notebook. She wasn't planning to stay until the end, and Robbie had offered to drive her home.

'How did I do?'

'Let's see. With the first of these, the book and film have the same name, so that makes it easier. Yes to *Mary Poppins*. You've got *The Godfather* right. And wasn't Jay brilliant as Jo in *Little Women*? The film and book you didn't get, the one where you've just written *Rambo*, was called *First Blood*. So, no free tickets for you! Oh, I forgot, you paid for them in the first place, didn't you?'

23

Monday

"In the first week of July, a heatwave will bring sunshine and high temperatures across much of the UK. High pressure will build from the southwest, with clear skies and temperatures on the rise."

***

Ginny felt comfortable returning to her investigations. She had enjoyed the previous afternoon at the Rec, but now Adam had been discharged from hospital and was convalescing at home and Ginny looked forward to life returning to normal. She studied the photographs Adam had taken at the Abacus Accountants' office, starting with his photo of the desk. Ginny could visualise where she had seen the missing phone. It was just there, on the corner, next to the little stack of business cards, one of which Adam had picked up. There was a space there now. A box of paperclips had been knocked over, spilling its contents on the desk. Maybe there had been a struggle? One paperclip, straighter than the others, had travelled further and had come to rest on her own bookkeeping files. It reminded Ginny that she was pleased Stephen had agreed to take over her account. She decided to ring him.

'Abacus Accountants. How can I help you?'

'Hello, Stephen. It's Ginny; I hope you are settling back into the pace of Shepton Rise life. I wonder if you could help me with something that has been bothering me?'

'Sure. Go ahead.'

'It's about your brother's phone. I saw it on the desk during our appointment with him, and then Adam sent a WhatsApp message to it later, but the police didn't find it when they searched the room. It was quite a new one, wasn't it?'

'It certainly was. I was trying to nudge my brother

into the twenty-first century at last, so it was a present from me.'

'Am I right in thinking it was in a blue case? I didn't see the back of it.'

'Yes, that's right. I bought the case from a market in Newquay. It's turquoise on the back. The seller had customised it with a picture of a surfboard. Just my little joke. My brother was the last person I would have expected to see on a surfboard.'

'Actually, Adam and I were surprised that he had WhatsApp installed.'

'Me again! Guilty as charged. I downloaded it before I gave the phone to him. I used to send him photos of Cornish beaches.'

'Was he into the whole phone culture, using jargon and emojis?'

'Good God, no! He was very formal. I would ramble away about something, and he would reply, *noted*, or *precisely*.'

'Thank you, Stephen. By the way, Susan Cunningham-Hill is throwing a garden party to raise funds for the next Stage Centre production. I'll make sure you get an invite. You can network with the *ladies who lunch!*'

***

Ginny had left a voicemail for Julia earlier, and now Julia was replying.

'I spoke to Rupert, and he told me that it is possible to track a phone, even without a sim card, but it can be difficult. Generally, it needs to be connected to the internet.'

'Did he know of any places where you could sell a phone?' asked Ginny.

'There are many online dealers and auctions, but there would still be a trail back to the person who stole the phone. The first place he suggested you try would be *Bish-Bash Fast-Cash* in Cranthorpe.'

'Blimey! That's a mouthful!' commented Ginny.

'Apparently, everyone calls it *Bish's*. It's a pawn shop.'

'Thanks, Julia. I know just who to talk to next.'

***

It wasn't often that Steve came to Cranthorpe. Compared to most English towns, it was a very good place to live, but in comparison with the much smaller Shepton Rise, it didn't quite come up to the mark. The town planners had never been able to agree on the plans for a bypass, so as a result, traffic en route for the city often got snarled up on the high street. One or two buildings had been erected that were less than sympathetic to the surrounding historic environment. It was a wonder that some builders had got away with the alterations they had made, ripping out stone mullioned windows that had stood the test of time for two hundred years and replacing them with large softwood picture windows that would be lucky to last another thirty. However, Cranthorpe was home to several specialist shops not to be found in Shepton Rise, and Steve was standing outside one of these now; a lurid red and yellow sign proclaimed: *Bish-Bash Fast-Cash*.

As Steve pushed open the door, a bell jangled loudly, announcing his arrival. He paused a moment, firstly to let his eyes adjust to a room devoid of natural light after the bright sunshine outside, and secondly, because he couldn't think of who the man behind the counter reminded him of. He was dressed in black jeans and tee-shirt, and his long, black, greasy hair was combed back behind his ears. The man dragged his eyes away from his phone and scrutinised Steve. Then it dawned on Steve, *Ratso!* He looked like the character Dustin Hoffman played in *Midnight Cowboy*. Ratso looked Steve up and down. A lightweight, black zip-up jacket, blue shirt, black tie, grey trousers and, of course, those boots could only mean one thing - a visit by the police. Steve approached the counter. His expression was deadly serious, but in his mind, remembering a line from the film, he was saying, *I'm walking here, I'm walking here!*

'I want to see your mobile phones,' said Steve. It was more of an order than an enquiry.

'Everything is legit. Straight up, it's all above board. I get ID from the sellers, you know,' whined Ratso.

'What's your name?' demanded Steve.

'Enrico,'

'Well then, Rico. I'm not doubting your honesty. Where are the phones? I've seen the ones in the window. Not what I'm after. Where are all the rest?'

'In there,' said Enrico, pointing to a locked, glass display cabinet. Steve scanned them. It was easy to spot the phone he was after; it was the only one in a blue case.

'Open it,' Steve commanded. Enrico duly obeyed him, struggling to fit the key into the lock. Steve pulled a handkerchief out of his pocket, used it to pick up the phone, and flipped it over to look at the back. It was turquoise, decorated with a white surfboard. Steve reached into his pocket again, took out a clear plastic bag and dropped it in. 'This one.'

'I s'pose you are gonna be confiscating it. I got a livin' to make, mate.'

'Rico. Did I say I wasn't going to pay for it? How much?' asked Steve.

Enrico took a card from the display case, which showed the make, model number and price of the phone.

'I'll give you a ten per cent discount. No, tell you what, you can have it for half price,' stammered Enrico.

Steve nodded. 'You said you get ID from the sellers. Show me.'

'I photograph it and then print it out and write the date on it. It's got to be photo ID,'explained Enrico, searching through a filing cabinet and then placing a sheet of paper on the counter. Steve looked at it, smiled, folded it, and popped it into the bag with the phone.

'I'll have that. And I'll need a receipt to claim this back.' Steve counted out the cash for the phone, glad that he had withdrawn enough from the bank. He was surprised second-hand phones were so expensive. Given that every young person in the country had one glued to their hand, how could they afford it? He gave a nonchalant wave over his shoulder as he left the shop, feeling Enrico's eyes boring into him.

Good, thought Steve, *Bish bash bosh, it's time I got some nosh.* He had noticed a cake shop earlier. It didn't look a patch on *Heavenly Delight*s, but how would he know unless he tried it? As Steve crossed the road to the bakery, he couldn't resist saying:

'I'm walking here, I'm walking here!'

***

Enough of all this crime investigation, thought Ginny as she picked up the mail from the doormat. *After all, I've got a business to run as well as a theatre production to bankroll. It's such a nuisance for Stage Centre to have their assets frozen! I'll have to look into it. I feel I'm getting a little swamped by everything! Too many loose ends. Now then, what have we here? An invitation to Susan Cunningham-Hill's garden party. I suppose I should be pleased, but it's just something else to prepare for. I do hope Adam will be well enough to come with me, or else I may have to politely decline.*

24

Saturday

International Test Cricket.

England v Scotland:

Scenario: England will be bowled out for less than 100 runs

Odds: 2000/1

£10 bet placed   LOST

European Soccer Final.

Spain v England

Scenario: Both teams will miss their first two penalties in a penalty shoot-out.

Odds: 300/1

£20 bet placed   LOST

MLB Baseball.

Chicago Cubs v Cincinnati Reds

Scenario: Chicago Cubs pitcher will throw a perfect game and hit a home run in the same game.

Odds: 200/1

£30 bet placed   LOST

American Football:

Pittsburgh Steelers v Baltimore Ravens

Scenario: The Steelers will score a touchdown on every possession.

Odds: 150/1

£40 bet placed   WON

***

'I've something to announce,' said Adam.

'Announce?' queried Ginny, looking around the room, 'But there's only me here!'

'Wrong choice of words,' replied Adam sheepishly, 'Reveal? Declare? Divulge?'

'Why don't you just tell me?'

'Okay, well, as you may know, I've been spending a lot of time on the computer lately. I wasn't sure it would ever happen; it was stressful at times, but I rode my luck, and it paid off.'

'I have absolutely no idea what you are talking about!' laughed Ginny.

'All will be revealed, declared and divulged. The rewards are in my bag.'

'I wondered what was in that hold-all.'

'Ta da!' sang Adam as he pulled a sheet of paper from his bag. 'I can now announce, reveal, and declare that I have been awarded a commendation from an online photography foundation course, even if I did have to print out the certificate myself. It doesn't end there - cue drum roll - I can also announce, reveal, and declare that the Open University has accepted me on their Photo-journalism course.' Adam delved into his bag again and flashed his acceptance letter. 'So, all those long hours at the computer were worth it!'

'Well done, indeed!' said Ginny, applauding. 'It's quite a big bag for two pieces of paper.'

That's because I can announce, reveal, and declare that my savings account has reached its maturity,'

'Unlike you!' quipped Ginny.

'I shall continue, resume and carry on, despite the heckles. So, I cashed in my savings, and I bought these!' Adam reached into his bag again and held up a large digital camera in one hand and a long zoom lens in the other.

'Oh, well done you!' Ginny gave Adam a congratulatory kiss on the cheek.

'Thank you. Are we ready to party? I mean, ready to garden party!'

***

'What a beautiful garden,' exclaimed Ginny, 'It's a hidden gem!'

'I know,' replied Susan Cunningham Hill, 'So close to the town centre, yet you wouldn't know it is here. The lawns take a lot of upkeep, but my husband, Gerald, has a sit-on mower, and he enjoys bombing around on it. Actually, Charlie Dibbs from the Garden Centre has started to help with the mowing on the odd weekend.'

'I hope the weather holds up for you,' commented Adam, 'It's lovely and warm, but the weather forecast said we might get a thunderstorm.'

'If we do, we'll all be squashed together under the marquee. What fun! Go on down and join the others,' said Susan.

The first person they encountered was Robbie.

'Hello, son. You look like you are waiting for someone.'

'I was hoping that Laura was going to come. The

trouble is, I overheard Cassidy inviting her along to the Live Wire music festival, so that might have more of a pull than little old Shepton Rise.'

'Oh, that would be a shame if she didn't come. She's been so helpful to me. In fact, you both have,' said Ginny. *I'm going to keep my fingers crossed.* She thought, *It might make it a little hard to hold a glass of fizz, but it will be worth it if we get to see Laura again. I'm not sure I would recognise her out of uniform.*

'Is Lenny here?' asked Adam.

'I've not seen him. I know Susan invited him,' replied Robbie, 'What on earth is that racket?' A colossal, whirring, thumping vibration filled the air, as a helicopter swooped low and hovered over the garden before slowly descending and landing in the middle of the lawn. The doors opened, and two figures tumbled out, ducking below the swish of the blades as they ran towards the party. One of the men waved his arms at the helicopter, and it took to the sky and zoomed off.

'Hello,' said Ginny, 'You certainly know how to make an entrance!'

'You know me,' laughed Ricky Flynn, 'Anything to hog the limelight! Actually, my old friend Lenny here said he needed a new jacket and a flat cap. So we went to Savile Row to buy them. And I couldn't resist it, I bought one too!' Ricky donned his cap with a flourish, then arm in arm, he and Lenny strolled over to join the other guests, who greeted them with cheers and a round of applause.

'Who's this?' asked Ginny, seeing a young lady wearing a floral summer dress running down the path.

'It's Laura!' said Robbie with a broad smile.

'All right!' cried Adam, 'As the song says - Let's get the party started!'

***

Two things happened during the next few hours that would impact both the garden party and the murder investigations. The first was a whispered conversation between Ginny, Laura, and Robbie, and the second was an enormous clap of thunder, followed almost immediately by a downpour that had everyone racing for the shelter of the marquee.

It was a squash, but everybody appeared to be in good humour. Earlier, the members of Stage Centre had performed a medley from the previous season's musical, so now Julia switched the microphone back on, and, of course, *Singing in the Rain* was belted out by all the guests. Then, to everyone's surprise, Lenny stepped up and gave a beautiful rendition of *Danny Boy* in a clear tenor voice.

One person detached from the hilarity was Ginny. She was taking slow deep breaths and had to remind herself not to hold her glass so tightly.

'Are you alright,' whispered Adam.

'Yes,' she replied. 'Don't worry. I'm not going to have a panic attack. I guess it's time for me to step up!'

25

Saturday

'Hello,' said Ginny nervously. 'I'm afraid I'm not used to being this side of a microphone, and I wasn't sure if I should do this, or even if I could do it, but I decided there was no time like the present.'

'Hush!' hissed Angie to a few people still chatting at the back of the tent. She guessed something important was going to happen.

Ginny glanced around and saw that everybody she wanted to be present was here. Only two people,

Robbie and Laura, standing near the entrance, had the slightest inkling of what would happen next.

'First of all, at the risk of sounding like a church minister, I would like us to remember two people who can't be here this afternoon. Many of you will have known them better than I did: Matthew Walker and Graham Smith.' A murmur spread around the marquee as the guests either paid their respects or explained to others who the two men were. Ginny held up her hand to silence the crowd.

'Hush!' yelled Angie.

'Matthew and Graham,' Ginny repeated. 'The reasons why they were taken from us have been shrouded in mystery, and I have been trying to fight my way through the fog to the truth. I must admit, for a long time, I was completely lost.

Matthew was a man of many talents, but, like all people, he had his flaws, and many people held a grudge against him. That being said, I could not fathom how any of his faults could drive someone to commit murder. It was only after Graham Smith was killed, and I turned my attention to solving that mystery, that pieces of the jigsaw began to fall into place.

'Some of you may know that Adam and I were probably the last people to see Graham alive, apart from the murderer that is, and if it was not for that visit to his office and our subsequent return to meet Graham's brother, I would not have been able to make connections between the two.' There was a gasp as the implication of this sank in. Ginny took a moment to seek out Stephen Smith and nodded a solemn greeting. 'Yes, the two murders are connected. I had an instinct that something had changed in Graham's office, and when I studied before and after photographs of it, I realised that one of the files was missing. The accounts for Stage Centre!' Julia noticed all the members of the theatre group look at each other with apprehension and distrust. She saw Jay mouth, *OMG!* Angie was taking a keen interest in Jack's reaction - concerned about the force of his temper once it was aroused.

'I should share with you the fact that Adam received an emoji sent in a message from Graham's phone shortly after our meeting. After talking to Graham's brother, Stephen, we have concluded that the murderer must have sent it. Overconfidence, recklessness, or pure arrogance? Call it what you will, but it was an action that pointed me in the right direction. Graham's phone went missing from the office after his murder, and I'm certain the murderer took out the SIM card so it couldn't be tracked.'

Graham's phone went missing from the office after his murder, and I'm certain the murderer took out the SIM card so it couldn't be tracked.' Ginny spotted Julia's son Rupert in the crowd. His mother had managed to persuade him to leave his bedroom and show his face in the community. 'Rupert, tell me, how do you take a SIM out of a phone?'

'It's easy; the phone comes with a pointy thing that you push into a hole in the side.'

'And if you haven't got one of those to hand?'

'Oh, I just straighten out a paperclip.'

'Exactly. Adam's later photograph showed just such a paperclip on the desk, and thanks to Rupert's suggestion, Steve Green found the phone in Cranthorpe.'

'At Bish's?' asked Rupert. Ginny nodded and continued.

'How do I know it was Graham's phone? Firstly, it had a distinctive cover, which a market trader in Cornwall had customised. Maybe that in itself isn't proof, but, I've found out some new information today,' Ginny paused and made brief eye contact with Laura, who smiled in return, 'Although the murderer had wiped the phone to clean off fingerprints, it had a screen protector that Stephen had fitted before he gave the phone to his brother.' Ginny looked over to Stephen for confirmation.

'I tell you, it was a right palaver putting it on and not getting any air bubbles. It was off on, off on!' Stephen chipped in.

'And in doing so,' continued Ginny, 'Invisible to the eye but protected by the cover, Stephen had left a fingerprint. So today, I learned that it could only have been Graham's phone.' There was a murmur of excitement in the pavilion. 'But there is more!' Ginny held up her own phone. 'Where is the hole to take out a SIM, Rupert?'

'It's on the side of the phone. A little tray pops out, but you have to take off the cover first.'

'Exactly, thank you, Rupert. That is exactly what the murderer would have done in the office. Then, when he wiped the prints off - and I can tell you now that it was a he.' Ginny paused again, relishing the suspense of the moment. Julia noticed that both Samantha and Ashley were edging away from Jack and Chris. 'When he wiped the outside of the phone, he forgot that he had taken the cover off, and I have learned that the police found a perfectly preserved fingerprint inside.' Ginny sensed movement within the marquee, 'So, who will be the first person the police check? Another smug, overconfident mistake the murderer made was that the ID provided when he sold the phone at Bish's was a library card in the name of Philip Larkin.' Ginny pointed, 'There is the murderer, Patrick Martin!'

There was a collective gasp as Patrick burst through the crowd and dashed out of the marquee and across the lawn. The rain was still beating down furiously, and Patrick made slow progress on the soggy grass. Robbie and Laura looked at each other; Robbie raised an eyebrow as if to say, *Really?*'

'After you?' said Laura with a smile.

'Okay, I'll be happy to,' replied Robbie, 'I think he's had enough of a head start.'

It didn't take long; an out-of-condition librarian was no match for a young, fit Detective Constable, and Robbie quickly caught Patrick up. Adam captured the whole chase using his telephoto lens, including an excellent series of pictures of Patrick tripping and flying through the air to land sprawling on the wet turf. These were in sharp contrast to photographs of Ginny and Laura, the rain bouncing off their umbrellas, as they strolled leisurely across the lawn to witness Robbie making the arrest.

'Patrick Martin. I'm arresting you for the murder

of Graham Smith. You do not have to say anything, but it may harm your defence if you do not mention something when questioned which you later rely on in court...'

26

Saturday

Most of the guests had either gone home or called in at The Red Lion, all buzzing with excitement and in varying states of dampness, depending on whether they had been caught in yet another thunderstorm. Robbie and Laura were now on their way to City South Police Station with their prisoner. Rupert was back in the refuge of his bedroom, sending news of the arrest around the world using every social media application known to man or boy. Adam had rushed home to email his photographs to the major news agencies - his first photojournalist scoop. Ginny knew he would return to her side as soon as he had finished. Several guests, including the Dead Actors, the remaining members of Stage Centre, and Stephen Smith, stayed on, and Susan Cunningham-Hill had ushered them into the Orangery and was now serving them tea. Once everyone was settled, Ginny began to speak again.

'Actually, I have to admit, I told a little fib,' she said with a giggle, 'I have no idea if Patrick's fingerprint was inside the phone cover. I just wanted to see if he would crack and admit his guilt by running.'

'But why did he do it? How did you know?' asked Samantha.

'Patrick was trying to cover up the fact that he had spent all the money in Stage Centre's bank account. When Matthew got wind of this and demanded an explanation, Patrick killed him. Then, when Graham requested a meeting to discuss the theatre company's finances, he killed him too, disposing of all the records. I belatedly realised that the police wouldn't have frozen the company's assets. They would only have done that if they suspected the money was profits from an illegal activity. Patrick's problem was there were no assets!

Then, a little birdie told me about the recent

computer survey that the Town Hall carried out on the Library's network. The issue, thankfully, was not of a sexual nature, but was the excessive use of online gambling. Many of the sites were accessed at times when the Library was closed to the public. Patrick was addicted to gambling!'

'And so, as the crimes were linked, you thought if you solved one crime, the police would follow up the other,' said Angie. But when did you suspect him?'

'I knew it was him when Laura sent me screenshots of who visited Abacus before we did. It was Patrick. He must have hidden upstairs, and later, after he had strangled Graham, he left by unbolting the back door. I just hadn't figured out how to catch him out at that stage. I didn't have enough hard evidence to contact the police.'

'I'm so glad he's been safely put away,' said Ashley. 'But the trouble is, we haven't got a theatre company anymore.'

'Nonsense!' burst out Julia. 'You are the people who matter. The play is coming along really well. I've already demoted Doc to understudy because you are making such good progress, Chris. The tickets and posters are in place for a glorious production. Then, next year, why don't you set up a new company?'

'Might I interject?' said Susan Cunningham-Hill, 'I would love to get involved. I had a career in PR and marketing before I married Gerald, and I'm sure he would be happy to help with the business side of things.' Then she whispered, 'In case you haven't guessed, he's got pots of money.'

'Hey, look,' cried Adam, who had just arrived back and was pointing to the sky. 'It's a rainbow.'

'Yes,' said Doc, 'If the sun is shining and it's been raining, you can bet there's a rainbow somewhere.'

'We'll have no more betting, thank you very much!' replied Ginny reprovingly.

'Well, they say there's a crock of gold at the foot of every rainbow. If I'm not very much mistaken, it's landed on the Red Lion,' remarked Steve, 'And last time I was in the pub, the brewery had just delivered an excellent guest ale called *Midas Touch*. Anyone fancy a pint? We should get Lenny to sing another song. His voice is pure gold!'

The End

A Note from the Author

Love a good mystery? Ready to dive deeper into the *Shepton Rise Murders*? Each book is a standalone story, available in paperback, ebook, and audiobook formats.

In the first book, *Murder Unscripted*, Ginny must overcome her fear of leaving the house—with support from Adam and, of course, the fun-loving Dead Actors—as she's drawn into solving the murder of one of her clients.

Murder in Focus follows Ginny and her friends as they struggle to unravel the mystery behind a shocking murder during a youth club photography session.

This is only the start—many more mysteries lie ahead!

You can order my books from Shopify, Amazon and most online retailers by visiting: www.stuckdave.co.uk While you're there, join my mailing list for updates on upcoming releases—and a chance to win free goodies!

I would love it if you followed me on Instagram: @stuckdavewrites Finally, I would really appreciate it if you could write a review of my book on Amazon. Even if you did not buy this book yourself from Amazon, you should still be able to post a review there.